GW00793128

Thank You For Your Application

Kevin Daughtry is bored. After writing over three hundred letters he has finally landed a really boring job in a really boring warehouse with a really boring boss. The firm has a new vacancy, and it is Kevin's job to reply to the letters that come in. In spite of an inner voice whispering 'careful', Kevin can't resist the personal approach, or suppress his sense of humour. The self-satisfied prig gets a put-down, the atrocious speller gets a rocket, others get helpful and sympathetic letters because he knows how they feel. The letters relieve the boredom, but they infuriate the boss when he hears about them. To make matters worse, Kevin is using office time and stationery to indulge his own passion for writing short stories. He knows his days at the warehouse must be numbered, but he doesn't really care. Above all an optimist, Kevin is sure that fame and fortune are out there somewhere, waiting for him.

Thank You For Your Application

John Kirkbride

ANDRE DEUTSCH

To Lynne

First published in 1989 by
André Deutsch Limited
105–106 Great Russell Street, London WC1B 3LJ

British Library Cataloguing in Publication Data

Kirkbride, John
  Thank you for your application.
  I. Title
  823'.914[F]

ISBN 0 223 98446 1

Printed in Great Britain by
Ebenezer Baylis and Son Limited, Worcester

uninteresting, unexciting, slow, dragging, flat, stale,
humdrum, dreary, depressing, jejune, wearisome,
monotonous, unentertained, unamused, browned off,
cheesed off, discontented, weary, jaded, indifferent,
satiated, cloyed, sick and tired, fed up, bored. . . .

Dear Diary,

Woke up this morning with a terrible hangover. Tried to get some sympathy off Mum at breakfast, but she cuffed me on the back of the head and said it was my own fault, which I suppose it was. Nobody *forced* me to drink eight pints of Lowerbrow Lager. On the other hand, nobody told me that NASA use it as space shuttle fuel. GOD it's strong stuff! After the fifth pint I told myself I'd better not have any more, but by then I was too drunk to listen.

We were out celebrating with Melvin Snetterton. His dad has just been released from Boltham Infirmary psychiatric wing, and his old firm have just picked up a massive order from Libya, so they've offered him his job back. Melvin's dead chuffed and grinned all night. His dad's company make pallet racking and storage equipment, and even when I said the Libyans probably wanted it for storing chemical weapons, it didn't seem to bother him. He just said 'Probably', and carried on grinning. If he keeps on smiling at everyone like that, they'll stick *him* in the psychiatric wing!

We saw Rachel on the way to Chuzzlewit's. She's looking quite well and said she was very happy, but she's had her hair cut short and put some weight on. Can't say I fancy her much anymore. Still, it was good while it lasted.

Work was a drag today. In fact, work's a drag *every* day. I've been at the warehouse for exactly a year tomorrow, and to be honest, I'm getting bored with it. It's not that I can't do the job, because I can. I was made Assistant Manager after only seven months, so I must be *fairly* good at it. It took The King (my boss, Elvis Jones), three years to get to be Ass. Man. Mind you, he's a right know-it-all, and what's worse, he smells.

Gets right up everybody's nose, ha ha. Someone should creep up and whisper BO in his ear, or buy him some deodorant or something. Come to think of it, he could've had some of mine. I got four gift packs of the stuff for Christmas and I haven't opened any of them yet. They've all got names like STUD and TOUGH GUY, but smell really sweet and sickly, like bathrooms after women have just come out.

Anyway, I was talking about work, (though GOD knows why). It's really beginning to get me down. It was better when I was just a labourer, messing about with the other lads and throwing boxes of beans and dried milk around. At least it was good fun, listening to their dirty jokes and weekend stories. Now all I seem to do is file delivery notes and answer the telephone, and they're making me go on a one day a week Management Training course, so I have to learn all about these boring things called Industrial Logistics and Occupational Incentives. De-reary. I admit, I don't know what an Industrial Logistic *is*, but it sounds pretty dull.

The next two weeks will probably be even worse. Jubbies (Jubilee Stores) have advertised for a Warehouse Assistant, (Kenny Mitchell got the boot for driving the stacker-truck over Elvis's foot), and I've got the job of replying to all the applicants again. The letters have already started coming in, and they're even talking about letting me do some interviews. I can't see it though, not if The King has anything to do with it. He's hated me right from my first day here, just because I giggled when he said he was called Elvis. It was me who gave him his nickname. Actually, I hope they *don't* let me do interviews, as I'd probably pick someone for their sense of humour, then they'd turn out to be lazy, or a thief or something, and we'd *both* get the sack.

Anyway, I've been getting back into writing just recently, and I'm working on another short story. The last few I've sent out have been rejected, but the editor of

2

one magazine was quite encouraging, and said I had some 'weird and wonderful ideas'. I sent him a story about this big multinational company discovering an ancient lake, and using it to make Primaeval Soup which they sell in cans, but all the un-formed creatures in it suddenly evolve when they're heated up, and jump out of the pan and strangle all the housewives. I think I may write to Joyce Beckett who was in my class at school. She was dead brainy and went to college to do A-Levels, and is doing an English Degree at Canterbury now. She may be able to give me some advice. Plus, she's fit.

I've got to do something though. I've decided that working in a warehouse is not for me. I'm bored. I'm fed up with being an insignificant Assistant Manager. I've got something to say, (I think it's called the 'creative surge'), and I'm going to say it.

I just hope somebody out there will listen.

Mon. 8th February '88.

To: Jubilee Stores,   Fri. 5th February '88
      151 Meed Lane,
      Rushfield,
      Nr. Boltham.

Dear Sir,

I am writing in reply to your advertisement for a
Warehouse Assistant at Jubilee Stores. I am 24 years old,
and have been working as a counter assistant at Lomas
& Crook's travel agents for the last three years. I am
quite skinny, but I am stronger than I look, and I think I
would be able to do warehouse work quite well.

My reason for leaving the travel agents was because I
wanted to work in a warehouse.

Yours sincerely,

John Cabot.

To: John Cabot,   Tue. 9th February '88.
    14 Ameryk Close.
    Boltham.

Warehouse Assistant

Dear Mr Cabot,

Thank you for your application for the above post.
We have had many letters, and I'm sorry to say that on this occasion, you have not been picked for our shortlist for interview.

However, I would like to thank you for your interest, and wish you success with any future application you may make.

Yours sincerely,

Kevin Daughtry

Ass. Warehouse Manager.

To: Jubilee Stores,   Fri. 5th February '88.
    151 Meed Lane,
    Rushfield,
    Nr. Boltham.

Dear Sir,

You have advertised recently in the BOLTHAM
EVENING CHRONICLE for a Warehouse Assistant. I
am sixteen years of age and live with my parents just off
Boltham Road. I have two CSE's and would like to come
in for an interview for the job, as this is the kind of work
I have been looking for.

Yours sincerely,

Kenneth Cheeseman.

To: Kenneth Cheeseman,
    23 Limburg Drive,
    Boltham.

Tue. 9th February '88.

Warehouse Assistant.

Dear Mr Cheeseman,

Thank you for your application for the above post.

We have had lots of letters, and I'm sorry to say that on this occasion, you have not been chosen for our shortlist for interview.

However, I would like to thank you for your interest, and wish you success with any future application you may make.

Yours sincerely,

Kevin Daughtry

Ass. Warehouse Manager.

To: Jubilee Stores,   Fri. 5th February '88.
    151 Mill Lane,
    Rushfield,
    Nr. Boltham.

Dear Sir,

    With regard to your recent advertisement for a
Warehouse Assistant, I would like to apply for the job. I
am 45 years old, active and single, and have had Manuel
jobs all my life.
    If you are holding interviews, I would be pleased to
come in and see you at your convenience.

                        Yours sincerely,

                            Arnold Bottoms.

To: Arnold Bottoms,   Tue. 9th February '88.
    56 Croup Street,
    Assheton,
    Nr. Boltham.

Warehouse Assistant.

Dear Mr Bottoms,

Thank you for your application for the above post.
We have had scores of letters, and I'm sorry to say
that on this occasion, you have not been picked for our
shortlist for interview. I'm afraid your experience as a
Spanish waiter may have proved of little practical value.

However, I would like to thank you for your interest,
and wish you success with any future application you
may make.

                    Your sincerely,

                    Kevin Daughtry

                    Ass. Warehouse Manager.

P.S. Why do you want to be interviewed in the toilet?

To: JUBILEE STORES,   Sat. 6th February '88.
    151 Meed Lane,
    Rushfield,
    Nr. Boltham.

Dear MR. JUBILEE,

    I am writing in REPLY to an advert I saw in the
BOLTHAM EVENING CHRONICLE for the job of
WAREHOUSE ASSISTANT at JUBILEE STORES. I
am SEVENTEEN, I have TWO O LEVELS and I am
unemployed at the moment.
    Please would you send me an APPLICATION FORM
as I would like to apply for the job.

             Yours sincerely,

               MICHAEL LONDON.

To: Michael London,   Tue. 9th February '88.
      Robert's Hotel,
        New King Street,
      Boltham.

Warehouse Assistant.

Dear MR LONDON,

    THANK YOU for your APPLICATION for the above POST.

    We have had HUNDREDS of LETTERS, and I'm sorry to say that on this OCCASION, you have NOT been picked for our SHORTLIST for INTERVIEW.

    HOWEVER, I would like to THANK you for your INTEREST, and wish you SUCCESS with any FUTURE APPLICATIONS you may MAKE.

                  Yours sincerely,

                  Kevin Daughtry

                  Ass. Warehouse Manager.

P.S. You didn't need to SHOUT!!

To: Jubilee Stores,   sat. 6th February '88.
       151 meed Lane,
          Rushfield,
             Nr. Boltham.

Dear sir

   I am riting in repli for your advertisement in the
Boltham evening chronicle for a warehouse assistant.
Altho I am a gril, I am very strong and can litf boxes as
wel as boys.
   Cud I have a intervu for the jod as I am quit kean to
work and an at the momt unemploid.

                     yours sincerely,

                        Phyllis Tyne.

To: Phyllis Tyne,   Tue. 9th February '88.
    261 Green Street,
    Boltham.

Dear Phyllis,

I'm sorry to tell you that you have not been chosen for interview for the position of Warehouse Assistant. We have had hundreds of applications and were really looking for someone with experience. (Apart from which, my boss would kill me if I invited a bird in)!

Also, you were in my year at school so I know who you are, and I'm quite sure you would not be suitable for the job. We would prefer someone who has taken the trouble to learn to read and write. However, I must congratulate you for your inertiative in using your poor letter writing to highlight the fact that you come from a bad family, and so make me take pity on you. Unfortunately for you I am not easily fooled, and even people with rotten parents can spell the word 'girl'.

In any case, you're far too skinny, and I doubt if you would be able to lift a box of matches, let alone a box full of tins of Heinz Space Invaders.

Sorry I can't be more helpful.

Yours sincerely,

Kevin Daughtry

Ass. Warehouse Manager.

To: Kevin Daughtry,   Thu. 11th February '88.
    c/o Jubilee Stores,
    151 Meed Lane,
    Rushfield,
    Boltham.

Dear Kevin Daughtry,

I have just seen the letter you sent to my daughter concerning the job of Warehouse Assistant, and am left almost speechless by your disrespect and impertinence.

For your edification Mr Daughtry, here are a few facts.

First of all, Phyllis has probably put more effort and hard work into learning to read and write than you will ever put into anything, and it is a testament to her dedication and perseverance that she has achieved as much as she has. My daughter happens to be dyslexic.

Secondly, she does not in fact come from a 'bad family' as you suggest. On the contrary; my husband has his own highly successful printing business, whilst I am a lecturer in adult education at Boltham Technical College, and we both strongly resent the implication that we are 'rotten parents'. We are not.

Finally, the fact that my daughter was 'skinny', (as you so tactfully put it), was due primarily to acute depression, which occurred as a direct result of her schooldays having been made a complete misery by people such as yourself, who persisted in teasing and tormenting her until she was so unhappy, she couldn't eat. Since leaving school she has blossomed, and it may interest you to learn that the enclosed photograph of a fine, healthy looking young woman, is a recent one of my daughter, Phyllis.

In future, you would do well to keep your opinions and

suppositions to yourself, or at least get your facts straight before you put pen to paper.

Yours indignantly,

Inez Tyne.

To: Inez Tyne,   Sat 13 February '88.
    261 Green Street,
    Boltham.

Dear Ms Tyne,

I am writing to apologise for my comments about your daughter, Phyllis. I think you are absolutely right when you say I should get my facts straight before putting pen to paper. I'm afraid this is a fault of mine, and in the past, I have almost been thumped for opening my mouth before putting my brain in gear. I do hope Phyllis wasn't too upset by my letter, as she always seemed such a nice girl at school.

By the way, you are quite right about the photograph of Phyllis. She certainly is a fine and healthy looking young woman, and that little white bikini suits her a treat. Perhaps I could call round and take her out for a drink one night, to make up for my being so rude in my letter? Do let me know.

Once again, I apologise for my tactfulness, and look forward to hearing from you.

Yours sincerely,

Kevin Daughtry

To: Kevin Daughtry,   Mon. 15th February '88.
    c/o Jubilee Stores,
    151 Meed Lane,
    Rushfield,
    Nr. Boltham.

Dear Mr Daughtry,

Phyllis is currently engaged to an electrical engineer
from Manchester, and is very happy.

I would appreciate it if you would refrain from coming
anywhere near this house, and I will thank you not to
write to either Phyllis or myself again.

Yours sincerely,

Inez Tyne.

To: Jubilee Stors   mon 8th february 88
    151 meed Lane
    Rusfield
    Nr boltham

dear sir

i writing for the job of werehouse assisstent that you
advetise in the paper i ave just leff boltham compriensive
skool an i sixteen year old i would like this job becos i am
unimployd an must arn some dosh for beer money i am
sixteen an singel and ave 2 cse in woodwork an
mettlework i will come in for a intervu if you want

your sinseely

M T Head

To: M. T. Head,   Wed. 10th February
      Flat 148,
         Eccles House,
         Boltham.

Dear Mr Head,

Thank you for your 'letter' regarding our vacancy for a Warehouse Assistant.

However, before I can make a recommendation for our interview shortlist, I need a little more information, and would like you to answer the following questions.

a). Are you dyslexic?
b). Were you bullied at school?

I would be grateful for your reply as soon as possible.

Yours sincerely,

Kevin Daughtry

To: Jubilee Stores,   Fri. 12th February '88.
      151 Meed Lane,
         Rushfield,
         Nr. Boltham.

deer Kevin Daghtry.

i am reply to your letter abowt the job of werhouse assisstent that you send me i am not dyslexic and i woz not bullid at sool as i never went i ope this is alrite

your sinseely

M. T. Head

17

To: M. T. Head,   Mon. 15th February '88.
    Flat 148,
      Eccles House,
      Boltham.

Dear Mr Head,

Whilst I have almost every sympathy with you for your lack of education, I'm afraid that you have not been picked for our shortlist for interview.

Personally, I don't think that being illiterate is a crime, (and you certainly don't need to be a genius to do this job)! but if I invited someone in for an interview and my boss found out they couldn't spell, he'd give me the sock.

Sorry I can't be more helpful.

Yours sincerely,

Kevin Daughtry

Ass. Warehouse Manager.

To: Jubilee Stores,   Tue. 9th February '88.
      151 Meed Lane,
      Rushfield,
        Nr. Boltham.

Dear Sir,

    I have just seen your advertisement for a Warehouse Assistant in the RUSHFIELD ADVERTISER, and I would like to apply for the position. Although I happen to be a girl, I don't feel this would be a disadvantage, and am quite sure I could do the job just as efficiently as any boy – more so than some I know!

    I am 19 years old, 5' 6" tall with red hair and green eyes, and have 5 0-Levels and 2 A-Levels. I play badminton and swim regularly, so I am quite athletic and feel that unloading and stacking boxes should present no problem. I am at present unemployed and would be happy to come in and see you about it.

    I look forward to hearing from you.

Yours sincerely,

Marci Niland.

P.S. I have never applied for a manual job before. If you ask me in for an interview, should I come smart or casual?

To: Marci Niland,   Thu. 11th February '88.
    9 Oban Avenue,
    Rushfield,
    Nr. Boltham.

Dear Marci,

Thank you so much for your lovely letter which I received today. I must complement you on your handwriting – cartography happens to be a particular interest of mine.

Anyway, down to business. We have had a tremendous amount of applications for the job we advertised, and as Assistant Manager, I've had a heck of a time sorting through them all, I can tell you.

However, I'm delighted to be able to tell you that you have been chosen for our shortlist for interview, and if it's at all convenient, we would like you to come in and see us on Wednesday, 17th February. If this date does not suit your current timetable, please let me know straight away, and I'll try and arrange an alternative meeting.

Till then – ora voi!

Yours sincerely,

Kevin Daughtry

Ass. Warehouse Manager.

P.S. Something like a denim mini-skirt and fitted white tee shirt would be fine for the interview. We're not formal here!

Dear Diary,

What a boring week. It seems ages since I wrote in here, but it was only last Monday. Six days! It feels more like a month. I've answered hundreds of applications for the warehouse job! Well, maybe not hundreds, but a lot. Well, about nine actually, although two of them were to the same person and one was to Phyllis Tyne's mother. You wouldn't believe some of the plonkers who're writing in! I thought *I* was bad, but they make me look like Shakespeer. Mind you, Phyllis Tyne turned out to be dyslexic, and I got a really snooty letter off her mum about the reply I sent. I felt pretty bad about it afterwards, but these cheeky comments keep jumping onto the page, and I don't seem to be able to stop them. I think there must be a gremlin in the typewriter. Still, I shouldn't take it out on some poor sod just because he can't spell. Who needs to spell to stuff boxes on shelves, anyway? I really must try to stop taking the piss.

The best letter I've had so far was from a girl who said she had red hair, green eyes and an athletic body, so I've invited her in for an interview. The King will probably go bananas now because I've asked a girl in for a labourer's job, but I don't care. If he says anything, I'll stuff the Equal Opportunities Handbook up his bum!

I couldn't get the front door open this morning for all the Valentine's cards piled up behind it. Well, slight exaggeration – I got *one*. Mind you, I only *sent* one. It was to Melanie Wilson who works in the wages office at Jubbies. She's really nice, though I don't know whether my mum and dad would approve if I brought her home. She's coloured. Not really what you'd call black – more a sort of milk chocolate brown, but I think she's dead pretty. The nice thing about her is, she doesn't seem to notice that she's a different colour to everyone else at Jubbies. She's just dead normal and chatty, and even *I* forget what colour she is when I'm talking to her. (Not that I'm indiscriminate anyway). Her hair's quite long and straight, and she always has yellow ribbons in it tied with bows, (like in the Old Oak Tree). I think she's great.

Anyway, I sent her this card with a picture of a little man on the front saying, 'I'd like to bring some colour to your cheeks', then inside it shows him looking really lecturous and spanking this naughty schoolgirl who's over his knee. I signed it 'From a secret admirer'. I hope she doesn't guess it's me. But then if she doesn't, there won't have been much point in sending it, will there? But if she does . . . Oh bugger it.

The one I got has 'I'm not a girl of easy virtue' on the front, then inside it says 'But don't let that stop you trying!' It was signed 'From a dark horse', but I don't recognise the writing so I've no idea who it's from.

I'm going to use the typewriter at work tomorrow to write a letter to Joyce Beckett (the girl at Canterbury University) about my literary career. I think I'll send my latest short story along as well to give her an idea of my style. Probably all I need is a little help with my grammer and things, like that. I'm quite sure I've got enough imagination. Then if I can make some money from writing, I'll be able to give up this measly job at the warehouse and become famous! They might even have me on Wogan! I hope Sue Lawley's doing it that week.

I suppose I'd better go and have a bath now. I might even open one of my gift packs of talc and aftershave. I could wear some tomorrow and see if Melanie likes it. If the Denim advert is anything to go by, she should be all over me!

Sun. 14th February '88.

To: Joyce Beckett,   Mon. 15th February '88.
    36 R. D. Laing St.,
    Canterbury.

Dear Joyce,

You may not remember me as I was shorter then, but I was in your fifth form class at Boltham Comprehensive in 1984. I know it's a long time ago, and that I once lifted your skirt up in the playground with a slide-rule, but I think old school friends should keep in touch, so I hope you don't mind me writing to you now. It's no use crying over a lot of water under the bridge, as they say.

The main reason for my letter, is that I need some advice from someone who is good at English. I am quite good at English myself of course, but because I was busy working, I didn't have time to go to College like yourself and study the subject further. Unfortunately, as I have decided to become a writer, I feel this gap in my education is holding me back.

What I really need are some hints on things like plot, characterisation and style. I have sent some short stories out to various magazines, but they don't seem to be quite what they're looking for. I wondered if you could give me some tips on what sort of subjects people are interested in, and also, what are the things editors look for when reading a short story?

I have enclosed my latest piece of work to give you an idea of how good I am. I hope you will be able to find time to help me in this matter, and look forward to hearing from you.

                        Yours with best wishes,

                        Kevin Daughtry

P.S. Do you still wear those knickers with the little blue flowers on?

The Girl with the Long legs.

David Watson was bored. He was bored with his job, bored with his girlfriend and bored with life in general. In fact, he was bored with everything, (except Egypt, although he had never been). He sat in the restaurant with his coffee cup in front of him, and the remains of a Tortellini in Cream Sauce and a large Praline Bombe on his plate. The Bombe, (moulded strawberry and vanilla ice creams with almond praline centre, decorated with vanilla flavoured whipped cream and strawberries and topped with a rich chocolate sauce – serves 6), had been deliceous, but he was even bored with that. Life just seemed to be one long toll. If only someone interesting would ring.

As David paid the waitress, (Sheila, a blonde with blue eyes and too much make-up), he happened to glance out of the window into the street, whereabouts he saw something that made his heart stop. Well, nearly, because if it had stopped completely he would have fallen off his chair and died, which would certainly have made the meal a waste of money, ha ha. What he saw was a girl, but this was not just any girl. *This* girl was something else man! She wore a short, stone-washed denim mini-skirt and a tiny white top which showed off her midrift, but what really caught David's attention, (and made the waitress wince with envy), were the girl's legs. The girl's legs were the longest, smoothest, brownest, most perfect legs he had ever seen on a girl.

The girl tossed off her head and flicked her Titian (bright golden aubern) hair out of her face, and caught sight of David, sitting gobsmacked in the restaurant and staring at her. She flashed him a tantalating smile, then within seconds, she was lost in the crowd. David leapt to his feet as if he'd sat on a barbeque, and almost knocked the dirty plates out of Sheila the waitresses hand who was holding them.

'Oy, watch it creep!' she said, in her strong Lancashire accent.

'Sorry,' said David, 'But I have to go.'

'Eee, you're all the same you blokes,' Sheila said, with her arms akimbo and folded in front of her, 'You'll chase anythin' in a skirt.' David tipped her a wink, (though she would have preferred money, ha ha), and streaked out of the restaurant into the maddening crowd.

David was twenty five years old, tall and fair haired, and though he was a bit short sighted, he wore soft contact lenses which he didn't have to take out every night. He was a nice chap, though recently he had been losing his temper more, mainly because he was bored with his job. The problem was, David wanted to be a painter, but no one would accept his paintings, so he was forced to make a living by working in a Do-It-Yourself store, where he spent all his time doodling on the rolls of wallpaper.

Anyway, pushing his way through the milling thongs he peered in front of him, hoping to catch sight of the incredible girl with the long legs, but all he could see were other people who weren't her. He stopped for a minute and stood on his tiptoes and glanced across the road, and spotted the girl just going into the tube station at Old Holborn. He dashed up to some traffic lights and pressed the button, and the light lit up and said 'wait'. He watched without any patience as the little red man changed to a little green man, and even before the beeping had started, he rushed across the road and down into the tube station.

When he reached the bottom of the huge escalator, he looked around him, desperately seeking Susan, (for that was the girl's name, though he only found this out later), but the girl was nowhere to be seen, and then he saw her. She was just disappearing into the station marked Baker Street, and smiling inside himself to himself, David thought, 'Hmm, I could *do* with Sherlock Holmes's help on this one.' He ran after the girl as fast as he could run, which wasn't very fast because of the crowds of people, who all seemed to be going in the opposite direction to Martin.

Finally, as he leaped onto the platform, he was just in time to see those beautiful long legs getting aboard a train, (not the girl – just the legs, ha ha), and he dashed through the doors just seconds before they wheezed shut behind him. As the train pulled off, Martin began to make his way towards the front where he had seen the girl get on. At last, after about five minutes, he spotted the girl up ahead through the doors between the carriages, and heaved a sigh of relief. Then he heaved a sigh of nervousness. What was he going to say to her? How was he going to introduce himself? 'Hello. I've been stalking you around the city because I lust after your body. Will you go out with me?' No, that wouldn't do. She'd probably run away and call the police. Perhaps he could put it better. 'Hello. I've followed you across half of London because I think you've got the most incredible legs I've ever seen. Can I buy you a drink?' That sounded better, but she would still think he was some kind of weirdo. London is full of them.

Suddenly, the train pulled to a stop suddenly, and Martin fell into the lap of a middle aged woman who was knitting some bootees, and one of the needles went up his nose. When he looked up, the girl was gone. He dashed off the train and stared around the platform, but there was no sign of her. He ran off the platform and along the corridor and up the huge escalator, and stood panting at the top. He glanced for a long time around the ticket office, but there wasn't any trace at all whatsoever of the girl. She had disappeared, as if up her own bottom. Martin shrugged and resigned himself, and his shoulders drooped in disappointment. Slowly, like a man who has just been sacked, he made his way out of the station.

As he stepped out onto the pavement, a low, husky

voice said, 'Hello, looking for me?' Martin glanced up in surprise, and there, standing by the railings, was the girl with the long legs, smiling at him as if they were old friends.

'But . . . but . . .' he stammered, and the girl laughed, for she had a sense of humour.

'I know you've been following me because I saw you. Now I want to know why.'

'Oh, er, well, it's embarrassing really,' said Martin, who was really embarrassed.

'That's allright,' said the girl, 'I'm not shy.'

'Well,' said Martin, summonsing up all his courage, 'I think you've got the most incredible legs I've ever seen, so I followed you.'

'Thank you for the compliment,' said Susan, 'My flat's just around the corner. Would you like to come in for a drink?' Martin didn't need asking twice, and before you could say Jack Robertson, they were round at Susan's flat having a drink.

After they had been to bed, Susan made some cappachino coffee and put a drop of Remimartan brandy in it, and they sat sipping it on the settee. Susan smiled at Martin with a mouthful of coffee.

'Do you know what?' she said, swallowing the coffee first.

'What?' Martin asked, furloughing his brow.

'I'm glad you followed me,' Susan said.

'So am I,' said David, and they both guffawed brightly.

The End.

To: Jubilee Stores,   Tue. 16th February '88.
     151 Mill Lane,
     Rushfield,
      Nr. Boltham.

Dear Sir,

I am writing about the advertisement in the
RUSHFIELD ADVERTISER for a Warehouse
Assistant, as I would like to apply for the job. Since I
don't know whether or not tha needs me to fill in an
application form or owt, I thought as how I ought to say
a bit about my sen.

I went to school at Boltham Council School and
started work at 14 as a labourer with a building firm.
Since then, I've done pretty well owt tha could mention
so far as employment goes, including a fair crack as a
warehouseman. I am smart and presentable, and am free
to come in for an interview any morning tha fancies.

I look forrard to hearing from you.

                    Yours faithfully,

                       Fred Higginshaw.

To: Fred Higginshaw,   Thu. 18th February '88.
    528 Huddersborough Road,
    Boltham.

Dear Mr Higginshaw,

Dream on.

For a start, no one under the age of 60 uses words like 'tha', 'forrard' and 'owt', and I don't think anyone under the age of 60 is called Fred either, (apart from Janice Long's little boy). I also happen to know that Boltham Council School became Boltham Secondary Modern in the mid 1940's, and since 1965 it's been Boltham Comprehensive. And I don't know how many years it has been illegal to leave school before age 16, but it's more than *I* can remember.

The top and bottom of it is Fred, I think you're too old. I also think this is a shame, because I'll bet you're dead honest, trustworthy and hard working, and if I had my way I'd give you the job. But if I did that they'd fire *me*. You know how it is. My boss just wouldn't wear it, and he's a miserable bugger at the best of times. I'm sorry I can't be more helpful.

Perhaps you could try gardening. According to this magazine I read, it's one of the most satisfying and rewarding pastimes known to man. I know it's not like a job, but if you grew vegetables or something, perhaps you could sell them on the market and make some money.

Anyway, whatever you decide to do, good luck!

Yours sincerely,

Kevin Daughtry

Ass. Warehouse Manager.

To: Kevin Daughtry,   Sat. 20 February '88.
    c/o Jubilee Stores,
    151 Meed Lane,
    Rushfield.

Dear Mr Daughtry,

    Thank you for your kind letter which I got today. Tha's quite right about my age – I'm 65 and have been forced to retire. Seems bloody daft to me. I'm still a damn sight better worker than these young whippersnappers they're employing nowadays.

    Anyroad, thank you for writing back – most folk don't bother – and good luck tha sen.

                    Yours faithfully,

                      Fred Higginshaw.

P.S. I've been gardening for forty year, but I appreciate the suggestion like.

To: Jubilee Stores,   Thu. 18th February '88.
    151 Meed Lane,
    Rushfield,
        Nr. Boltham.

Dear Sir,

I am writing in reply to your advertisement in the
BOLTHAM EVENING CHRONICLE for a
Warehouse Assistant. I'm sorry the letter is a bit late,
but we don't get the Evening Chronicle at our house, and
I only saw the advert as I was looking through an old
copy at my girlfriend's whilst waiting for her to get
ready.

Anyway, I am 19 years old and went to school at
Greenmill Secondary. I have four O-Levels, (English
Lang, Geography, Woodwork and Metalwork), and one
CSE in History. I live with my mum and dad in
Greenmill, and I am unemployed at the minute, but this
is because I was on a Government Training Scheme and
they didn't give me a job at the end of it. They said they
would, and then when it came to the crunch they decided
they didn't need me anymore, and took on another
Training Scheme lad instead.

I can come in for an interview any day except
Saturday and Sunday, when I stay at my girlfriend's
house. (She has a place of her own). I am very keen to
get the job and I also have some experience, as the job I
had on the Training Scheme was in a warehouse at a
woollen mill.

                    Yours sincerely,

                    Chris Stevens.

To: Chris Stevens,   Mon. 22nd February '88.
    13 Pickwick Lane,
    Greenmill,
    Nr. Boltham.

Warehouse Assistant.

Dear Chris,

Thank you for your application concerning the above post.

I am glad to say that you have been chosen for our shortlist for interview, and we would like you to come in and see us at 9-30 am on Friday 26th February.

If this date is not convenient, please let me know as soon as possible, and we will try to arrange an alternative meeting.

                    Yours sincerely,

                    Kevin Daughtry

                    Ass. Warehouse Manager.

To: Jubilee Stores,   Sat. 20 February '88.
    151 Meed Lane,
    Rushfield,
    Nr. Boltham.

Dear Sir,

As I was walking past the Job Centre the other day on my way to a business meeting, having a few minutes to kill, I decided to call in out of curiosity. It was there that I spotted your advertisement for a Warehouse Assistant, and I must say, I found it rather interesting. Whilst I am probably rather over-qualified for the job, it is exactly the sort of thing I have been looking for.

In loo of a full Curriculum Vitay, (my only copy was accidentally thrown away by our housekeeper), I shall give you a brief rundown of my qualifications and experience.

I was educated at Manchester Grammar School where I got nine O-Levels and four A-Levels, wheretofore I proceeded to Trinity College, Oxford, where I gained a First in Histrionics and Sociology. Since then, I have spent my time preciously, doing a variety of jobs to give me as much experience as possible. I have been a teacher, an engineer, a social worker, a male nurse, a computer operator, a milkman and a warehouse assistant. But of all the wide and various positions I have held, I must say that the job of warehouse assistant was my favourite, and that is the reason I am applying for the job at Jubilee Stores. It sounds right up my street.

I think my past experience should suit the job perfectly. As a teacher and a social worker, I learned all about how to deal with other people's problems, which should come in very useful. Also, if someone happened to fall off a high shelf or something and hurt themselves, I would be able to use my experience as a male nurse and bandage them up. My computer knowledge would be dead useful for any office work I might have to do, and having once worked in a warehouse, I've got a pretty good idea of what the script is. I suppose my experience as a milkman won't be much use really.

Anyway, if you are still holding interviews, I should be glad to come in and have one at any time. I am twenty years old and of smart appearance, and I think I would be a great assit to your company.

I look forward to your repose.

Yours sincerely,

Barry Munchausen.

To: Barry Munchausen,
     369 Rodomont Road,
     Franklin Heath,
     Manchester.

Tue. 23 February '88.

Dear Mr Munchausen,

Thank you for your application. Your letter sounded strangely familiar.

However, due to the fact that every single person in the world applied for the job, we have only been able to invite a fraction of them in for interview, and unfortunately, you have not been picked for our shortlist.

With so many people to choose from, we decided to go for somebody with two brains, who could use a computer keyboard with one hand whilst typing out a goods invoice with the other at the same time, which as you can imagine, saves greatly on office staff. Also, we needed someone twelve feet tall so we could get rid of the stacker-truck.

I'm sorry I can't be of more help to you, but might I suggest you get in touch with NASA, who I believe are looking for new astronauts at the moment.

Yours sincerely,

Kevin Daughtry

Ass. Warehouse Manager.

To: Kevin Daughtry,   Thu. 25th February '88.
    c/o Jubilee Stores,
    151 Meed Lane,
    Rushfield.

Dear Mr Daughtry,

I think you're taking the piss, and I also think you're out of order.

Okay, I admit that I might have exaggerated a bit in my letter, but that only goes to show how much I want the job. People like you make me sick. You're safe in your nice little job with your weekly wage packet, and you've got no idea how it feels to be out of work. I've written over two hundred letters in the past year and NOT ONE firm have invited me in for an interview! You don't know what it's like not being able to afford to go out with your mates, or buy the new Deacon Blue album, or take your girlfriend to the pictures. I'll tell you what it's like. It's CRAP!

You should try it sometime, then maybe you wouldn't be so ready to laugh at other people's misfortunes.

Up Yours sincerely.

Barry Munchausen.

36

To: Barry Munchausen,
369 Rodomont Rd.,
Franklin Heath,
Manchester.

Mon. 29th February '88.

Dear Barry,

Good for you!

If nothing else, your letter of 25th February shows you, have spirit!

I'm sorry if you found my letter offensive, because believe me, I do know how it feels. Before I got this job, I was unemployed for over two years and wrote more than 300 letters. I've papered one wall of my bedroom with them! So I know what it's like to be skint, and I know what it's like not to have enough money to take your girlfriend out. (I split up with mine because of it). You might be surprised to learn that some of my own applications were a lot like yours.

Anyway, I'm afraid you were too late for the warehouse job, but if you're still interested, Jubilee Stores will be advertising for a stacker-truck driver next week. (The guy who took over recently was always pissed and kept crashing, so they've put him on sales). If you have a driving licence or any experience, why don't you apply for the job? (Only this time, tell us what you're *really* like).

Best wishes and good luck.

Yours sincerely,

Kevin Daughtry

Ass. Warehouse Manager.

To: Jubilee Stores,   Wed. 2nd March '88.
      151 Meed Lane,
      Rushfield,
      Nr. Boltham.

Dear Sir,

I believe you are advertising for a Stacker-Truck
Driver, and I would like to apply for the job.

I am twenty years old and went to Franklin Heath
Secondary School. I have three O–Levels and two CSE's.
Since leaving school I have done a Trainee Management
course at a pea factory, and had a Saturday job in a do-
it-yourself store. I passed my driving test after having
lessons with my uncle, who is a driving instructor.

I can come in for an interview at any time, and I look
forward to your reply.

                    Yours sincerely,

                        Barry Munchausen.

To: Barry Munchausen,   Fri. 4th March '88.
      369 Rodomont Road,
      Franklin Heath,
      Manchester.

Dear Barry,

Thank you for your application.

I am glad to say that you have been picked for our shortlist for interview, and we would like you to come in and see us on Friday, 18th March.

If this date is not convenient, please let me know as soon as possible, and we will try and arrange an alternative meeting.

Yours sincerely,

Kevin Daughtry

Ass. Warehouse Manager.

To: Kevin Daughtry,   Wed. 2nd March '88.
     391 Boltham Road,
     Boltham.

Dear Kevin,

Thank you for your letter of 15th February; it was certainly a surprise. I do indeed remember you, and I'm glad to hear you've grown taller. I also remember you lifting up my skirt in the school playground, and should we ever meet again, I would advise you not to repeat this overtly sexist prank. I am a member of the Women's Action Group here who run courses in unarmed combat, and I am now quite adept at inflicting severe damage to a man's more vulnerable regions.

I was very interested to read your short story, THE GIRL WITH THE LONG LEGS. However, if you're really serious about having decided to become a writer, I'm afraid the story leaves much to be desired. You have an awful lot to learn. (Perhaps you should have paid a little more attention in school).

To begin at the beginning, I have to say that the very title itself is pretty dreary. It's too simplistic; too pedantic. What you should do, is take some interesting facet of your story and incorporate it in the title. Since you're talking about legs, think shape, texture, colour. A good example is the Strangler's song, 'Golden Brown'. Or if you particularly wanted it to describe the action, you should have been a little more enigmatic and called it something like, STALKING THE FLESH.

I'm afraid your style is also far too prosaic. It has no poetic rhythm or metre. Of course, this wouldn't necessarily be a bad thing if the content were strong enough to carry it, but unfortunately, it isn't. If you're going to use this kind of simple, Hemingwayesque language, you have to include some kind of underlying message or moral. Failing that, the piece should stand as an example of brilliant prose, in which case the 'story' is less important.

(Incidentally, a good story should have a powerful beginning, a strong middle and preferably, some kind of twist at the end).

Quite apart from this, we're never particularly interested in the characters or what happens to them, because they are completely two dimensional. I mean, what do we know about David? That he's 25, tall and fair haired, short sighted and a frustrated painter. It just isn't enough to go on to form an objective opinion about whether or not we like him. As for the girl, all we know about her is that she has nice legs and is a victim of male chauvinist subjugation.

Good characterisation is essential if we are to empathise with the people in the story. Max Perkins once said of Fitzgerald, that he had 'the quality of being able to note a point of character and then make a general observation with some wit, and yet make it a part of the fabric of the prose'. In other words, you, don't suddenly stop the action simply to indulge in a brief description of the character. The description should be an *integral part* of the action. EG: 'His cornflower blue eyes darted nervously across the street.' The action doesn't stop, but now we know what colour his eyes are. And by the way, try using rather more interesting names. You appear to have found David's so boring, that halfway through the story you forgot what it was and changed it to Martin!

Finally, I felt I had to mention the subject matter, which was so ludicrously sexist and so typically male, it would have been funny were it not so offensive. You just cannot write about women as if they are mere accessories to the perpetration of visual rape. We are not simply bowls for the rotten fruit of man's lust. Women are people, individuals, with strong minds and strong bodies, and deserve to be treated as such.

Last but not least, watch your spelling, and try to

avoid writing 'ha ha' at the end of every funny line; it's not necessary. I also strongly advise that you invest in a copy of Roget's Thesaurus, which I think you will find invaluable. It'll help you avoid repetition, and should improve your descriptive powers considerably.

I hope this letter will be of some help to you as a writer, and if you need any more advice, don't hesitate to drop me a line. (I've included a list of books you ought to read below).

Nice to hear from you after all this time, and good luck.

Ciao,

Joyce.

P.S. Yes, I still wear the knickers with the little blue flowers on, but not the same pair I hasten to add.

Recommended Reading

Under the Volcano	Malcolm Lowry.
Howard's End	E. M. Forster.
Murder in the Cathedral	T. S. Eliot.
The Soft Machine	William Burroughs.
Ulysses	James Joyce.
The Caucasian Chalk Circle	Bertold Brecht.
The Rainbow	D. H. Lawrence.
Nostromo	Joseph Conrad.
Waiting for Godot	Samuel Beckett.
Six Characters in Search of an Author	Luigi Pirandello.
Remembrance of Things Past	Marcel Proust.
Death in Venice	Thomas Mann.
The Women's Room	Marilyn French.

To: Joyce Beckett,   Mon. 7th March '88.
   36 R.D. Laing St.,
   Canterbury.

Dear Joyce,

Thank you very much for your letter which came last Friday. I was a bit surprised to hear that you didn't think much of my story, but I have taken notice of your advice, and I think my latest piece is much better. I spent nearly all weekend on it, and I have paid strong attention to the things you mentioned, such as style, plot, characterisation, subject matter and names.

Also, on my way home from work on Friday, I bought one of those Roget's Thesaurus things (they're not cheap are they?!) and it's brilliant. It took me a while to figure out how to use it, (my mum sussed it in the end), but now, I don't know how I ever managed without one. It's got some really awesome words in it!

Anyway, I went out on Friday night and got slightly bibulent, so I didn't get much writing done on Saturday morning, but by teatime I was really racing along! I've put the story in with my letter for you to look at, and I'm sure you'll agree that it's a big improvement on THE GIRL WITH THE LONG LEGS. I was so naive when I wrote that.

Well, that's about all for now. I hope you enjoy the story and look forward to hearing from you soon.

                    Best wishes,

                    Kevin Daughtry

P.S. Hope you like the powerful beginning and the twist at the end. You will also notice that I've given the woman the stronger character this time, to avoid subjugation.

P.P.S. What does 'ciao' mean?

43

Suddenly, the man jumped off the train and flew through the air like a piece of paper, with his clothes flapping in the wind like bits of rag. He landed with a bump that nearly shook his bones out of their sockets. He rolled down the embankingment, and bits of gravel went in his knees and made his hands bleed like stuck pigs. Eventually, after falling for quite a long time, he stopped at the bottom and looked up at the train, which sped off on its way to London.

Back on the train, Dulcibella looked out at the countryside which whizzed past the window. For a minute, she felt like the train was standing still, and the scenery was travelling backwards, like in the old movies where the fields were made of canvas fastened to a big cylinder which spun round.

Her emerald green eyes peered about her at the other passengers, and she shook her strawberry blonde hair out of her pulchritudinous face. Her small mouth smiled as she noticed a little boy, picking his nose and flicking the bogies at a man in a bowler hat. The little boy was called Siegfried, but his mother was reading a Mills and Boon and didn't seem to notice. Dulcibella glanced across to the other side of the compartment, not meaning to see anybody, and suddenly she saw a man. He was dressed casually in jeans and a Genesis sweatshirt, and his hair was long and blonde but well kempt. He was reading 'The Caucasian Chalk Circle' by Bertold Brecht, and his face looked deep and inexorable.

Dulcibella's heart missed a beat, for she thought she had never seen such an attractive man. If he had been a woman, she would have said he was beautiful, but he wasn't so she couldn't. But he was certainly dervishly handsome. He glanced up suddenly and his deep lapsis lazuli eyes caught hers. It was too late to look away, because then he would have realised that she didn't mean to be looking at him, so she kept her eyes where they were and flashed him a callipygian smile.

For an infinitesimal moment, the man looked confused, then gathering himself together, he smiled back at Dulcibella. She noticed that his teeth were straight and not crooked, and also, she noticed the way some small wrinkles came out from the sides of his eyes, which made him look even more attractive than ever. Dulcibella took a deep breath and summonsed up her bottle.

'Do you mind if I join you?' she said. The man shifted uncomfortingly on his seat and his face suddenly raddled. Dulcibella smiled inwardly at the thought of the power she held over him. It made her feel powerful. The man nodded clumsily, like a toy dog in the back window of a car.

'Er, n n no . . .' he stammered, his face still raddling even more.

Dulcibella picked up her briefcase containing all the things she used as a book illustrator in London, like pieces of paper, pens and suchlike, as well as a book she was reading on the mysteries of Egypt, and perambulated over to the seat opposite the young man. She sat down with another whining smile, and the young man grinned at her like a sheep.

'My name's Dulcibella,' she said, reaching out to shake hands with him.

'Oh,' said the young man, 'My name's Ichabod, but most of my friends call me Ichy.'

'Well, pleased to meet you, Ichy,' said Dulcibella shaking his hand, 'I hope *I* can be your friend too.'

Ichy smiled pleasantly, but Dulcibella could see that he was nervous, and this made her feel good. She was a person, an individual, with a strong mind and a strong body, and knowing that she made Ichy nervous made her feel even stronger still. She was not just an object of men's desires. In fact, men were the object of *her* desires.

Thinking this thought made her laugh out loud, though no one had said any joke. Ichy looked flummoxed and nonplussed.

'Why are you laughing?' he said, worried that he had egg on his chin or something. Dulcibella's eyes glistened omnivorously.

'Do you really want to know?' she said.

'Well, yes,' Ichabod said, 'You make me nervous when you laugh.'

'Don't be nervous,' Dulcibella said, placing her long slender hand over Ichy's hairy but tanned one, 'I'm not going to hurt you.'

'Weell,' Ichy said slowly, still a bit unsure about this strong, individual woman. Dulcibella squeezed his hand to reinsure him.

'Follow me to the loo in about five minutes,' she said, 'And I'll prove it.'

'Prove what?!' Ichy said alarmingly, thinking all sorts of thoughts.

'That I'm not going to hurt you,' Dulcibella said. She got up and perambulated sexily to the toilet, her lascivious bottom oscillating alluringly under her tight, faded Levi 501's, (with the original red stitching).

Ichabod, even as nervous and unsure of himself though he was, waited for five minutes, and then followed Dulcibella to the comfort station. He knocked timidly on the door, which opened from the inside, and a long slender hand reached out and pulled him into the cubicle. It was Dulcibella in there!

She pulled Ichabod close to her, (which wasn't difficult, ha ha), hitched up her denim skirt to reveal sexy black stocking tops, and began to undo his tie. He started to blush again, and had to hold onto the handle next to the toilet.

'I, I really don't know if we should be doing this . . .' he stammered, although he was really enjoying himself by now.

'Ssh,' Dulcibella said, 'I told you I wasn't going to hurt you,' and she silenced his quivering lips with some severe osculation.

Ichabod couldn't believe his luck as he walked back to his seat afterwards. Nothing like this had ever happened to him before. Still smiling with himself, he took out his Bertold Brecht book and continued to read.

Suddenly, the train came to a sudden stop, and Ichabod was thrown forward out of his seat and landed in the lap of the person sitting opposite. It was then that he woke up. His first thought was, 'Oh no! It was all just a dream!' He was so disappointed that none of it had really happened, that he felt like crying.

Just then, he felt a long slender hand on his shoulder, and a voice said, 'Don't worry Ichy, sometimes dreams come true.' Ichabod looked up at the person whose lap he had fallen into, and couldn't believe his eyes. It was Dulcibella! She licked her lips and smiled at him, and all of a sudden, he realised that she was right. Sometimes dreams *do* come true. They grinned at each other for a moment, then both started chuckling happily.

The End.

To: Jubilee Stores,   Wed. 9th March '88.
    151 Meed Lane,
    Rushfield,
    Nr. Boltham.

Dear Sir,

I have just been to the newsagents and bought a copy of the Boltham Evening Chronicle, which I like to read whilst I'm having my tea. I always have fish fingers, boiled potatoes and peas on Wednesdays, as I prefer to keep to a regular routine. Anyway, just as I was finishing my mug of tea, (I like to have a mug, because if I have a cup I find it's not enough and I have to have another one), I noticed your advertisement for a Stacker-Truck Driver, and it caught my eye immediately.

I have been out of work for one year, two months and thirteen days now, but the last job I had, (with Boltham Council Parks Department), was as a mowing machine driver, which is very similar to a Stacker-Truck Driver, as they both involve driving. (If you notice, both end in the word DRIVER). As a Mower-Machine Driver, my job was to drive a mowing machine over the grassy areas of the local parks. (The mower-machine cut the grass). Although I have never driven a stacker-truck, I am sure it is very similar to driving a mower-machine, and perhaps even easier in some ways, as I wouldn't have the problem of avoiding trees.

I am thirty five years old, five feet eight and a half inches tall and of medium build, (though I have put on some weight lately as I am very fond of Jaffa Cakes). My hair is brown and my eyes are also brown, and I went to school at Boltham Comprehensive and got two CSE's in Domestic Science and Geography.

I can come in for an interview any day except Thursday morning, because on Thursday morning I go and pay the rent for Mrs Barnes who lives on Liversage

Road, as she cannot get out of the house much anymore. She has arthritis and a bad knee, due to falling in the snow last January.

Yours sincerely,

Tom Petty.

P.S. I am not in fact the American pop star of the same name, though some people have said I look like him, apart from my face and hair colour.

To: Tom Petty,   Fri. 11th March '88.
      39 Fikey Lane,
      Boltham.

Stacker-Truck Driver.

Dear Mr Petty,

Thank you for your application for the above post, which arrived here this morning and which I opened with a ruler. The ruler was a twelve inch one made of see-through plastic.

Unfortunately, I have to tell you that you have not been picked for our shortlist for interview. The shortlist is typed on Croxley Script typing paper and pinned on a cork notice board at the back of the office. The office is decorated with woodchip wallpaper and painted in vinyl silk emulsion, and the colour is called Magnolia. (Which interestingly enough, is the title of a song by your American namesake). The secretaries seem to like the colour, though I think it's a little dull myself.

Anyway, I would like to thank you for your interest and wish you luck with any future applications you may make, (though not with us).

                    Yours sincerely,

                    Kevin Daughtry

                    Ass. Warehouse Manager.

To: Jubilee Stores,   Sat. 12th March '88.
     151 Meed Lane,
     Rushfield,
     Nr. Boltham.

Dear Sir,

I am writing about your advert for a Stacker-Truck Driver which my probation officer showed me. She said I should write to you about it, as it would be a good job for me and would keep me out of trouble. She said I should be completely honest in my letter, and this time, not say I have been working abroad. If you really want to know the truth, I've never been further than Butlin's in Skegness.

I have just come out of Strangeways Prison, where I have been serving 18 months for burglurry and assaulting a police officer. But I only burgled because I needed the money for my girlfriend's heroine, though she is off the smack now and has got a part-time job in a Chemist's shop. I hit the officer because he got in the way when I tried to run for it. I didn't mean to hit him, but he moved his head and it bumped into my fist as I ran past.

Anyroad, I have done my bird now and am trying to go straight by getting a job. If I had a job, I wouldn't have to go out and nick as I would have some honest dibs in me skyrocket.

Yours sincerely,

Dick Welsh.

P.S. Please could you send me a detailed layout of the building, as I have a very bad sense of direction and might get lost if I have to come in for an interview.

To: Dick Welch,   Tue. 15th March '88.
    Flat 5,
        Barlinnie House,
        Franklin Heath,
        Nr. Manchester.

Stacker-Truck Driver.

Dear Mr Welch,

Thank you for your application for the above post. I'm afraid your prison record doesn't look too good on a job application, does it? According to Melanie, (who works in the office here), we would need reports from Strangeways and a letter from your Probation Office before we could invite you in for an interview.

Though you said in your letter you were trying to go straight, I must say I found your request for a 'detailed layout of the building' a tad suspicious. What we really need is someone who will drive the stacker-truck *inside* the warehouse, as opposed to out of the loading bay doors and off up the street.

If you could submit the proper reports and things, we might be able to reconsider your application. Otherwise, I suggest that you get in touch with the Merry Men, (c/o Robin Hood, Sherwood Forest), as they may have an opening for you.

Thank you for your interest.

Yours sincerely,

Kevin Daughtry

P.S. Please don't come to the warehouse looking for me, as I don't work here anymore.

To: Jubilee Stores,   Wed. 16th March '88.
    151 Meed Lane,
    Rushfield,
    Nr. Boltham.

For the attention of the Managing Director.

Dear Sir,

I am writing to enquire about the job you advertised in the BOLTHAM EVENING CHRONICLE. I am a forty five year old housewife, but since your advert states that you are an Equal Opportunities Employer, I am sure this will not deter you from taking me on.

My youngest son and his wife have just emigrated to Australia, and have selfishly taken the baby with them, so there is nothing to keep me at home now. (My eldest son lives in Nottingham and has employed a local girl to babysit for him. *I'm* not good enough now he's become a Southener)! My husband is something of a lazy slob and hasn't worked in four years, so I decided I would go out and get a job myself.

As I can only type with one finger and do not do shorthand, office work is out of the question, so I am writing to you in the hope that you will give me the chance of an interview for your driving vacancy. Although I do not hold a current driving licence, (nor an uncurrent one), I have at least 15 years experience of manouvering a shopping trolley around Tesco's, and I feel this skill should prove very valuable. I have noticed whilst doing the buying in, that it is mostly the men who crash into things, and as I have never had a single bump in all these years, I feel that steering around the shelves in a warehouse would present no problem.

I await your reply with anticipation.

Yours sincerely,

Mrs Ann Grimshaw.

To: Mrs Ann Grimshaw,   Fri. 18th March '88.
    14 Sainsbury House,
    Boltham Road,
    Boltham.

Stacker-Truck Driver.

Dear Mrs Grimshaw,

Thank you for your application for the above post. Unfortunately, I must inform you that the vacancy has now been filled.

I'm afraid your experience on shopping trolleys in Tesco's may have proved of little practical value. Apart from which, there is no glove compartment on a stacker-truck, so you would have had nowhere to put your tissues, loose change, lipstick, Gold Spot, mascara, used car park tickets, Lil-lets, Polo Mints, petrol receipts, Woman's Own magazines, 10p off coupons, hairspray or spare pair of shoes.

Thank you for your interest however, and I wish you luck in finding a job. You'll need it.

Yours sincerely,

Kevin Daughtry

Ass. Warehouse Manager.

Dear Diary,

Another weekend almost gone and another boring week about to begin. I got a verbal warning off The King on Friday, because a couple of people have written in to Jubbies and complained about the replies I sent to their job applications. A few months ago I would have been worried sick about this, but I seem to have got to the point where I couldn't give a monkey's anymore. I'm so bored with this job, even the idea of going back on the dole doesn't seem so bad, (although I know it would be if I had to). I'm still taking the piss out of the applicants, even though I know I shouldn't, but at least it's something to do. I can understand some of the replies people sent to *me* now. They must have been naffed off with their jobs as well.

Actually, last week could have been worse. On Monday I finally found out who sent me the Valentine's Card, and it turned out to be Melanie from the office. It transpires (I got that word from my Thesaurus) that she's fancied me for ages but was too shy to say anything, and didn't think I fancied her anyway, and all the time I was thinking exactly the same thing! So on Friday night we went out for a drink after work, and we kept meaning to go home for tea, but we got on so well we kept having another one, and then another one, and eventually we ended up back at this flat that Melanie's looking after for this mate of hers who's on holiday. Then we found a bottle of vodka in the fridge, (though Melanie didn't want to drink it at first because it belonged to her friend), but it was only cheap stuff called Stoliknaya or something, so we necked it and ended up plastered.

Next morning we woke up in bed together, but neither of us can remember whether we did anything or not, and it was really embarrassing. I got a cab home and my mum nearly killed me because I hadn't rung to say I was staying out. She made me eat my tea from the night before, heated up in the microwave. It tasted like that pretend food they use on stage. Anyway, I haven't rung Melanie and she hasn't rung me, so I'll have to wait until tomorrow morning at work to see if we're still speaking to each other.

I sent another short story to Joyce Beckett a couple of weeks ago, but I'm still waiting to hear from her. She didn't think much of the first one I sent, but I must admit, the woman in it was very subjugated. I also went to the library and got out some of the books she suggested. I've already read Under the Volcano and have just started the Soft Machine. They're very interesting, although I must admit I was a bit disappointed with Under the Volcano. I thought it would be like a James Bond story, with an evil mastermind and a secret weapons factory hidden inside a mountain, but it wasn't like that at all.

Well, at least we've filled the stacker-truck vacancy. A guy called Chris Stevens got the warehouse job, and they took Barry Munchausen on as Stacker-Truck Driver. But then Jim (the van driver) left, so they put Barry on deliveries and stuck Chris in the stacker-truck. Now they're looking for a warehouse assistant again. I can't see us getting many applications though. It's only a few weeks since we advertised it before, so everyone's going to think it's a terrible job or something. Chris seems okay anyway, and we get on pretty well. He knows all kinds of stuff and is really into books, and says he'll lend me some. I'm going to be the most well read person in the warehouse!

Marci Niland – the girl who applied – came in the same day as Chris. Boy, did I get a rollicking for inviting *her* in, but it was worth it. She was absolutely gorgeous! 5′ 6″, green eyes, red hair and freckles right across her nose, and I'm sure she was wearing stockings. I felt all sad for an hour after she left. My GOD, those legs!

Well, that's about all for now as I must dash to the toilet. Back to the millstone tomorrow. Yuch!

Sun. 20th March '88.

To: Kevin Daughtry,   Tue. 22nd March '88.
     391 Boltham Rd,
     Boltham.

Dear Kevin,

Nice to hear from you again. I enjoyed reading your latest story, but to be honest, I think you may need more help than I can give. I'm afraid that – like most men – you seem to be obsessed with sex, and I'm sure you would do better to steer clear of the 'boy meets girl' scenario that you seem so fond of. Even though you've attempted to make the female character more assertive in this one, she is still ultimately no more than the object of the man's (admittedly latent) desire. I can't understand why your protagonists always have to end up bonking. You still seem preoccupied with the idea that women exist merely to please and titillate men, and that this is their sole motivation in life, and it may surprise you to learn that the exact opposite is in fact true.

However, I've listed below some of the points you should watch out for, in the hope that they may be of help to you.

1). TITLE/PROPER NAMES – The title doesn't seem to have anything to do with the story apart from trains, and 'The Six Fifteen to London' might actually have been more relevant. As for the characters, their names are certainly more interesting than in the last story, but they are unrealistic. I mean, come on Kevin, Ichabod?! The names should be unusual but believable. EG: Vladimir, Estragon, Lucky, Pozzo.

2). STRUCTURE – Whilst you've obviously taken my point about beginnings and endings, it would have been better if the exciting opening bore some relation to the rest of the story. What happened to the man who jumped

off the train? Why did he jump in the first place? Etc.
You can't simply introduce a character for effect, and
then completely ignore him; unless of course you have
some esoteric reason for doing so. I wondered if you were
hinting at a more subliminal theme, with mankind
(symbolised by the man) attempting to opt out of his
own destiny (symbolised by the train from which he
leaps).

3). CHARACTERISATION – Your characters are
slightly more rounded in the latest story, but they still
lack depth. Try making your dialogue a little more
informative in terms of what the characters are really
like.

4). PLOT – Slightly better, but again, nothing much
happens. I was still left feeling 'So what?'. If you're going
to write these simplistic narratives, your imagery, themes
and subthemes must be far more interesting.

5). STYLE – Again, slightly better, but you must be
careful when using your thesaurus. When you wrote that
Dulcibella 'flashed him a callipygian smile', I wondered
if you knew you were saying she flashed him *a smile with
well shaped buttocks*.

6). CONTINUITY – En route to the loo, Dulcibella
changes from Levi 501's to a denim mini skirt, and Ichy,
from a Genesis sweatshirt to a collar and tie. Was this
intentional? I wondered whether you were trying to
evoke a sense that people are somehow like chameleons,
never really showing their true colours.

7). HUMOUR – Finally, you really must try to avoid
following each funny line with the words 'ha ha'. This is
really the sort of thing that only the weird Kurt
Vonnegut Jr. can get away with.

I hope these pointers will be of some use to you, and if you decide to continue writing, I'll be glad to look at your next effort. Apart from getting a good laugh out of them, I use the stories as preparation for my Teaching with Analytical Subjectivity course.

No doubt I'll hear from you soon.

Ciao,

Joyce.

P.S. Ciao means hello or goodbye.

To: Joyce Beckett,   Sat. 26th March '88.
     36 R.D. Laing St,
     Canterbury.

Ciao Joyce,

Thank you for your letter of March 22nd. You certainly pulled my story to pieces, but this is just the sort of advice I need. From now on, I shall read all my work through when I've written it, so that I can correct my mistakes and continuity. I really am grateful to you for helping me in this way, as otherwise I would've had to go to nightschool, and I can't really afford it. I'm just glad that you're finding my stories instructive for your Teaching with Analytical Subjectivity course. It sounds great fun.

Incidentally, the reason my characters always end up 'bonking', is that I am aiming my work at the 'men's magazines' and that is what happens in those kind of stories.

Anyway, I have been reading some of the books you recommended, and also finding more new words in my Thesaurus, (though I look them all up now to make sure they don't mean 'well shaped buttocks' or something).

I agree with you about avoiding the 'boy meets girl' scenario, as I think this is rather played out now. If the books you recommend are anything to go by, people want to read more intellectual things, with strange characters, no story and lots of swear words. With this in mind, I hope you like my latest simplistic narrative, which is a story about two men with no women. I believe it has some interesting imagery, and I think it also has some good themes and subthemes hidden somewhere. I look forward to hearing your views on it anyway.

                    Ciao till then,

                    Kevin Daughtry

Street of Imagery

A Chinaman suddenly ran past at high speed and almost knocked them over. Vladivar and Tarragon watched him go, shrugged, and continued walking down the busy main street, which was choc-a-block with hoi poloi and ordinary people. They looked around them wonderingly. All around them were things to see. Interesting things and exciting things, and sometimes even horrible things. Because this was the City, the big, bad City, and the City is the place where things happen. The countryside is pretty boring really.

As they walked around the corner of a big stone bank, they almost tripped over something huddled up on the floor by the wall. At first, they thought it was an old Guy Fawkes dummy left over from bonfire night, but when Vladivar poked it with his stick, it groaned and moved and told them to piss off.

'It's a tramp!' said Tarragon.

'Yes,' said Vladivar, 'It's a tramp.'

'I wonder what he used to be,' said Tarragon, perusing up the tramp's tattered suit.

'Probably a banker,' said Vladivar. 'I expect he used to work in the bank here,' and he pointed at the solid stone walls of the bank with his stick to empathise the point, 'And then he stole some money and got put in prison, and now he's been reduced to this pathetic bundle of rags.'

Tarragon concurred.

'Yes. I expect that's what happened,' he said.

'Piss off!' said the tramp again, so they did.

Soon, they came to a cafe called 'Ken's Full Monty', and decided to go inside for a coffee and some doughnuts. They went inside and sat down. A chubby waitress with false blonde hair and a right rake of cheap make-up wobbled over to their table.

'Yeah?' she said, chewing and being cockney.

'We'd like two coffees and some doughnuts please,' said Tarragon.

'Doughnuts is off,' said the waitress, and scratched her bottom.

'Oh,' said Tarragon, 'Well, what have you got?'

'We've got turnover, tarts, flan, quiche, apple pie, gateau, sponge cake, cheesecake, fairy cakes, cup cakes, meringue, battenburg, eclairs, Chelsea buns, flapjack, brandysnaps, gingerbread, shortbread, garibaldi and custard creams,' said the waitress.

'But no doughnuts?' said Tarragon. The waitress gave him a terrible look and her butter-mountain make-up creased and crinkled.

'NO DOUGHNUTS!' she said, in a voice like GOD.

So Vladivar and Tarragon decided to have coffee and cheesecake, and the waitress brought them over and dumped the coffee on the table so that half of it spilled in the saucer.

'Thank you,' said Tarragon, but the waitress had waddled off to annoy someone else. They drank their coffee and began to dialogue.

'Why do you wear those little round glasses?' Tarragon asked Vladivar.

'Because I'm short sighted,' Vladivar told him. 'I didn't like wearing them when I was younger, but I kept bumping into things, and that's how I got this broken nose.'

'Ah,' said Tarragon, 'I've often wondered about that, because your ears are perfectly straight, so I knew you couldn't have been a boxer.' He ran his hand over his long, smooth face, with its pointed nose and nice grey eyes. 'Shall we go then?' he asked.

'Yes,' said Vladivar, wiping his round, stubbly chin with a hand, 'Let's.'

Back in the street, the two men began to perambulate again, looking around for more interesting sights to see. Suddenly, they walked past a huge shop window, and

Vladivar peered inside. In the window were lots of naked mannakins waiting to be dressed up in the season's latest stupid fashion. Vladivar stopped.

'Look!' he ululated, and Tarragon stopped too.

'What is it?' he said, squinting with appreciation at the shapely forms in the window, with their long, slim legs and perfect screw-on breasts, 'What's up with them?'

'Can't you see?!' said Vladivar, pointing and hopping, 'How subjugated they are!'

'Ah, of course,' said Tarragon, the penny finally dropping, 'Women, standing there naked in a shop window for all to see.'

'Yes! Yes! It doesn't matter that they're not *real* women.'

'No, of course not. Because they're *supposed* to be women, and that's just as bad.'

'Worse!' cried Vladivar in a passion, 'They're still subdued, vanquished, brought under bondage or into subjugation. Look! One's even got her arm missing!'

'You're right!' said Tarragon. 'It's a sad world Vladivar, a sad, sad world,' and they walked on down the street with legs bowed and heads hung low.

As they turned the next corner, they suddenly found themselves in a dingy backstreet, with boxes of rubbish piled up on the pavement and smelly steam coming from big tin things on the wall. It reminded Tarragon of when his dad used to park behind the Chinese restaurant when the family went for a birthday meal.

'It stinks here,' he said, sniffing the cabbagy air.

'That's because we're behind a Chinese restaurant,' said Vladivar, and he pointed to a name over a back door, 'Poo Man Pong'. All of a sudden, the same young Chinaman they had seen at the beginning came running from a door on the other side of the street, quickly followed by another Chinaman, who was welding a mashetti in his hand. He chased the younger man all the way up the street, and they disappeared around the corner.

'Triads,' said Vladivar.

'Probably,' said Tarragon.

As they walked on past a pile of rubbish, they noticed a scruffy looking dog with its nose buried in the mound of rotting food and vegetables. To the dog it was a feast, but then to a King, fish fingers, chips and peas would seem like rubbish, Tarragon thought thematically.

'He'd better not stay there long,' said Vladivar.

'Why not?' asked Tarragon.

'Because if the man with the axe comes back and sees him, there'll be Crispy Fried Dog on the menu tonight!'

'Lyerk,' Tarragon said, and shuddered, as he was quite fond dogs and had one of his own called Churchill. Then a rat suddenly dashed out from under a box and ran across the street, squeaking like some hinges. Tarragon shuddered again. He didn't like rats.

'Shall we get back to the highstreet?' he said.

'Good idea,' Vladivar agreed, and they made their way carefully back to the highstreet.

Back on the highstreet, the crowds were still pushing and milling and thonging, and the traffic was still farting carbon monoxide into the atmosphere. People in their houses were using deoderants and making holes in the ozone layer, and out in South America, they were still chopping down the rain forests for fun. What does anything matter really, thought Vladivar. We'll all be dead soon anyway.

Tarragon and Vladivar began to walk, but they had only gone a few paces, when a youth ran past and snatched the camera from Tarragon's shoulder. Tarragon world round and called out.

'Hey! Hey, stop that youth! He stole my camera!' But everyone pretended to ignore him, and within seconds the youth was lost in the crowds. Tarragon sighed and was philanthropical about it.

'I hope the little bastard falls and the lens breaks and slits his throat,' he said. 'He won't get much for it anyway. It was only a cheap instamatic.' Vladivar shook his head.

'What a world,' he said, 'What a world.'

'Have you ever been to Egypt?' Tarragon said.

'No,' Vladivar replied, 'Why?'

'Because I think I may go and book a holiday there tomorrow. I'm fed up with the City.'

'You'll have to buy a new camera,' said Vladivar.

'I'll get postcards,' said Tarragon, 'It's cheaper,' and they both tittered amiably, ha ha.

The End.

To: Jubilee Stores,   Wed. 30th March '88.
     151 Meed Lane,
     Rushfield,
     Nr. Boltham.

Dear Sir,

I am writing in reply to your advertisement for a Warehouse Assistant, which I saw in the paper the other night.

For the last seven years I have been a long distance lorry driver, but I have decided to get a job nearer home, as I have suspicions that my wife has been knocking off someone else whilst I am away. She denies it of course, but I'm not stupid. I came home unexpectedly one afternoon, and found her dusting the bedside table in a short frilly nightie. The bedroom window was open, (even though it was freezing), and later on, I found a pair of Y fronts in the rhododendron bush. I'll swear they're not mine, but my wife says she bought them for me as a surprise, and then lost them whilst she was gardening. I suppose it *could* be true, but I'm not taking any chances.

I can come in for an interview any day you like as long as it is in the morning, as my wife goes to flower arranging classes every afternoon, and someone has to see to the dog.

                       Yours sincerely,

                       J. W. Greenhorn.

To: J. S. Greenhorn, Fri. 1st April '88.
13 Patsy Street,
Boltham.

Warehouse Assistant.

Dear Mr Greenhorn,

Thank you for your application for the above post.

I am pleased to tell you that you have been chosen for our shortlist for interview, and we would like you to come in and see us on Monday 11th April, at 9-30am. If this date is not convenient, please let me know as soon as possible, and we will try and arrange an alternative meeting.

Incidentally, I hope you don't mind me saying this, but I'd keep an eye on that wife of yours if I were you. I don't want to sound as if I'm casting aspirations, but if she comes back from flower arranging classes looking all red and flustered with her clothes on inside out, I should definitely look into the matter. I'm only saying this because my mum does flower arranging, but *her* classes are only once a week.

However, thank you for your interest, and we look forward to seeing you on the 11th.

Yours sincerely,

Kevin Daughtry

Ass. Warehouse Manager.

To: Jubilee Stores,   Tue. 5th April '88.
    151 Meed Lane,
    Rushfield,
    Nr. Boltham.

Dear Sir,

    I am writing in reply to your advertisement in the
Boltham Evening Chronicle for a Warehouse Assistant.

                Yours sincerely,

                   Kurt Longhampton.

To: Kurt Longhampton,   Thu. 7th April '88.
    211 Clerihew Road,
    Boltham.

Warehouse Assistant.

Dear Kurt,

    Thank you for your application for the above post.
You haven't got it.

                Yours sincerely,

                Kevin Daughtry

To: Jubilee Stores,
    151 Meed Lane,
    Rushfield,
    Nr. Boltham.

Wed. 6th April '88.

Dear Sir,

With regard to your recent advertisement in the Boltham Evening Chronicle, I am writing to apply for the position of Warehouse Assistant.

Since I feel that a full C.V. might be inappropriate for such a mundane appointment, here are one or two salient points about myself.

I am twenty three years old and unmarried, (though I have an active sex life and the nickname 'Randy'!), and own a cottage in Greenmill. I left Platt Grammar School with nine O and four A Levels, and gained a First in Sociology at Leeds University. Since leaving the embrace of Alma Mater I have travelled widely, imbibing experience and cultural knowledge along the way. I now feel ready to settle down to some full time employment and a weekly wage, and since warehouse work is as good (I suppose) as anything else, I thought it might be fun to try it for a while.

If you wish to call me in for an interview, (though having perused my letter thus far, you may feel this is an unnecessary formality), I am free every day next week except Friday.

I trust your reply will be prompt, and look forward to hearing from you.

Yours sincerely,

Jeremy Pratt.

To: Jeremy Pratt,   Fri. 8th April '88.
    Burke's Cottage,
    Greenmill,
    Nr. Boltham.

Dear Mr Pratt,

Thank you for your application regarding the position of Warehouse Assistant. I trust this reply is prompt enough for you?

However, we have received the staggering sum of ONE other application for the job, and I'm sorry to tell you that on this occasion, you have not been chosen for our shortlist for interview.

The fact is Mr Pratt, we can very well do without your sort here, and I'm probably doing you a favour by rejecting you. Frankly, I don't think you would have got through the first day without someone punching your lights out. Alma Mater must have been pretty desperate, to go out with a dick like you!

Why don't you go off and become a brain surgeon or a nuclear physicist or something, and leave the 'mundane' work to us morons. Or doesn't a Sociology Degree cover things like that? I've been told they *give* them away, printed on toilet paper.

Once again, thank you for your letter, and as far as your 'active sex life' is concerned, bully for you. *My* nickname's Errol Flynn.

           Yours sincerely,

           Kevin 'In Like Flynn' Daughtry.

           Ass. Warehouse Manager.

P.S. Were you born with that surname or did you choose it specially?

To: Jubilee Stores,   Fri. 8th April '88.
     151 Meed Lane,
       Rushfield, Nr. Boltham.

Dear Sir,

I am writing in response to your recent advertisement in the RUSHFIELD ADVERTISER, for the position of Warehouse Assistant within your company.

I am a fifty two year old Senior Sales Executive by profession, but owing to circumstances beyond my control, I am forced to look elsewhere for employment. By rights, I should now be a senior partner in the firm of Cohen & Goldberg International Cosmetics, but I was unfairly passed over and elbowed out in favour of some young, financial whizzkid. The fact that his name was Silverstein didn't have anything to do with it of course, I *don't* think! They said they needed someone younger, with a new outlook and new ideas, and Silverstein was always full of new ideas. Absolutely brimming over with them he was. *My bloody ideas*!! Because the little bastard used to creep into my office at lunchtime and go through my Filofax and steal them! He thought I didn't know about it, but Janet, (my secretary, well, more than a secretary really), told me what was going on. So I hid behind my filing cabinet one day and caught him red handed, but when I told Cohen, he just laughed in my face and accused me of being paranoid. But like they say, you're not paranoid if they really *are* out to get you.

I digress however.

I should be obliged if you would invite me in for an interview at the earliest possible opportunity, since my redundancy money has all gone towards the divorce settlement with my wife, who left me when I lost my job.

My C.V. Is available on request.

                       Yours sincerely,

                       Randolph Hilter.

To: Randolph Hilter,
   33 Wakenfield House,
   Birchtree Gardens,
   Nr. Boltham.

Mon. 11th April '88.

Warehouse Assistant.

Dear Mr Hilter,

Thank you for your application for the above post. I'm sorry to say that you have just missed it, as the vacancy was filled only this morning.

As for the way you have been treated by your employer and your ex-wife, you have my condolences. It sounds as if you've had a pretty rough time of it, what with one thing and another.

Anyway, keep your double chins up, and I'm sure you'll find something in the not too undistant future. Thank you again for your interest, and good luck.

Yours sincerely,

Kevin Daughtry

Ass. Warehouse Manager.

P.S. Why not change the spelling of your surname and form a political party? You could go a long way.

To: Jubilee Stores,   Wed. 13th April '88.
     151 Meed Lane,
     Rushfield,
     Nr. Boltham.

Dear Sir,

I am writing in reply to your advertisement in the Boltham Evening Chronicle for a Warehouse Assistant.

Since leaving Hulme Grammar School in Oldham, (with five O and two A Levels), I have had a variety of jobs, including sales assistant, dyehouse worker, librarian, security guard, professional musician and painter & decorator, and I have twice worked in warehouses, once in a woollen mill and once at the Co-op Superstore in Oldham.

I am currently unemployed and most anxious to secure some form of regular income. Also, as an aspiring author, I have recently had my first novel (coincidentally, about someone who is unemployed) accepted by a publisher, but writing is not a get-rich-quick business, and I feel I need a sound financial base from which to pursue this career. I think the warehouse job would be ideal for me.

I would be most grateful for the opportunity of an interview, and look forward to hearing from you.

Yours sincerely,

John Kirkbride.

P.S. Travel would not be a problem, as there is a regular bus service from here to Boltham.

To: John Kirkbride,   Fri. 15th April '88.
    New Inn Farm,
    Highmoor,
    Nr. Oldham.

Warehouse Assistant.

Dear Mr Kirkbride,

Thank you for your application for the above post, but I'm sorry to inform you that the vacancy has now been filled.

However, I was very interested to hear that you are an author, because by a strange dint of coincidentalness, so am I! (though I haven't quite had anything published yet). I would be very interested to hear what kind of books you do, and if you would care to write back to me, I would be very grateful for any tips you could give me on how to get published. My own work is quite unusual, and of the Burroughs/Lowry 'Stream of Consciousness' school of thoughts.

Anyway, I'm sorry about the job, and perhaps we will meet one day at a literary bruncheon down in London.

Meanwhile, good luck with your career.

Yourd sincerely,

Kevin Corneleus Daughtry.

Ass. Warehouse Manager.

P.S. What kind of books do you read yourself?

To: Kevin Daughtry,   Mon 18th April '88.
    391 Boltham Road,
    Boltham.

Dear Kevin,

The stories are certainly coming thick and fast! I enjoyed reading STREETS OF IMAGERY, (though I'm still not sure about your choice of titles), and I definitely think you are improving. I have only one or two comments to make, and they are of a fairly general nature.

Firstly, forget the idea of sending your work to the 'Men's Magazines'. These perpetrators of filth and incitement to rape, are nothing but hypocritical sexist dross, and you should be aiming your stories at a far more intellectual market. You don't imagine people like D. H. Lawrence and Anais Nin sent their work to girlie mags, do you?

Secondly, there are still a number of glaring spelling mistakes which you must watch out for, and you appear to have used the wrong word on a couple of occasions, (unless of course this was intentional). Other than that, I can only stress again that for this kind of introspective narrative, your language and style need to be much more enigmatic, since, with no clear story involved, the interest lies purely in what you are saying and the way you are saying it.

Otherwise, I liked it, especially the concept of WOMAN as MANNEQUIN, and man's attempts to render her harmless (armless) by domination and naked display. There was some nice social comment there as well, with reference to the rain forests and aerosol deodorants.

I was also pleased to notice that, having used the Chinaman for your brisk opening device, you remembered to reintroduce him and explain his presence later in the story. You're definitely getting better.

Keep up the good work, and I look forward to your next piece.

Ciao,

Joyce.

P.S. You are still using 'ha ha' to emphasise humourous phrases. You really must stop this.

To: Joyce Beckett,   Fri. 22nd April '88.
     36 R.D. Laing Street,
     Canterbury.

Ciao Joyce,

Thank you very much for your comments on STREET OF IMAGERY. I was glad to hear that you think I'm improving, because *I* think so too. I'm sure that reading some of the more intellectual books you recommended has helped me a great deal, and you may notice in my current work, the strong influence of people like Burroughs and Beckett. (I have just finished WAITING FOR GODOT, and thought it was a scream).

I think my latest piece – IN AMONG THE PALET RACKS – is probably my best story so far. You will notice that it is a lot more serious than my other work, with many themes and subthemes and some interesting social comments. I have also taken your advice about enigmaticness, and I think you will find this one pleasantly puzzling. (And no subjugated women)!

Anyway, see what you think, and let me know when

you've read it. I shall look forward to hearing from you again.

Ciao,

Kevin Daughtry

In Among the Pallet Racks.

CHAPTER ONE.

Dunstan walked down between the lines of shelves, the lines of shelves that seemed to go on and on and on, as if they were going to go on forever. He peered about from side to side at the rows and rows of Heinz Baked Beans, Tetley Tea Bags and Bird's Instant Custard Mix. What did it all mean?

The gossamer blue strip-lights whistled overhead as his bulky grey thoughts whistled underhead, like a train somewhere, and he paused, scratching his tousledness, in front of the alcohol shelf. His porraceous green eyes wandered carelessly over the endless rows of bottles – whiskey, gin, vodka, martini, Jack Daniels, and a grin began to spread across his face even before he meant it to. Here was Heaven on a warehouse shelf, and who was to say that GOD himself was not in there among the bottles?

– Hello! Hello there GOD! he called out, laughing to himself as he did this, Come out, come out, wherever YOU are!

Macarius strolled down the isle whistling a tuneless tune by Madonna, and stopped in front of Dunstan. Dunstan carried on calling for GOD and laughing, crimson faced, dwarflike and huge. Macarius's eyes were wide with being open so far, and his mouth gaped like a pothole near Blue John mines.

– Where?! he cried, Where is GOD? Is HE there, in among the bottles?

– Oh yes, Dunstan said, nodding his head and wagging his finger, HE might be. Who knows where GOD might be?

– But in among the bottles? Macarius cried.

– Among them, or *in* them, Dunstan said, turning a knowing grin on his bemustered friend. Macarius's eyes opened even wider, and if it had been possible, (though it was not), they would have opened so far that they peeled right back over his head and he would have looked like a naked skull. A big white, gaping, moonless skull, glowering in rivers of really nasty stuff that stink to high heaven and are watching till whenever. But this didn't really happen.

Dunstan reached into the shelf and pulled out a bottle of Jack Daniels. He held the bottle in front of his face and peered in at the liquid. Then he put the bottle in front of Macarius's face and made him peer in at the liquid, slishing and sloshing in the bottle like bourbon. Macarius peered in.

– Can you see GOD? Dunstan asked him. Macarius peered even more, but there was no sign of GOD.

– I can't see HIM, Macarius said. I don't think HE's in there.

– Good! Dunstan shouted, Then we can drink the bottle.

CHAPTER TWO.

When they had drunk the bottle, they sat down *in among the pallet racks* and grinned at each other like soldiers who've survived. Their heads wobbled with car dogs window like in back, and bobbled like the wind with leaves. Their eyes were glazed as with pottery from a kiln, their vision like clay, giggling, giggling.

– Have you ever been to Egypt? asked Dunstan, slurring his words.

– No, Macarius said, slurring his, Have you?

– No. But I believe it's a beautiful country,

– Is GOD there?

– I don't know. HE might be.

– Does HE wear a hat?

– Only on Sundays.

– Is it a big hat?

– The biggest hat in the world!

– How big is that?

– Bigger than the pyramid at Giza.

– And how big is that?

– A bit smaller than GOD's hat.

– Oh, said Macarius.

He pondered with his thoughts for a moment, gazing at some packets of Homepride flour on the other side of the isle. The packets seemed to dance in front of his eyes, like pixies dancing round a mushroom in a forest on a moony night, but it was only pictures of Homepride men on the side, ha ha. He turned to Dunstan with his head still awobble, and hiccupped. Dunstan picked up the empty bottle of Jack Daniels and peered inside. He tipped it upside down and shook out the last few drops, then looked inside again.

– Any sign of HIM? Macarius asked.

– Who? Dunstan said.

– GOD.

– GOD?

– Yes.

– No.

– Oh.

There was a pause here where neither of them spoke. Then Macarius spoke.

– It doesn't look as if HE's in there then.

- No.
- No.
- No.
- It's a good job really, Dunstan said.
- Why? Macarius wanted to know.
- Because if HE *had* been in there, we'd have drunk HIM.
- Oh GOD! I never thought of that!
- And then HE would have been inside us.
- Yes!
- And if HE was inside us. . . .
- Yes?
- We would have been. . . .
- Yes, yes?!
- Outside him.
- And?
- That's it.
- Oh, said Macarius.

Just then, slithering like a long green snake through the long green grass, came Ronnie Monarch the foreman – king of the warehouse, ha ha. His evil black eyes peered about him evilly, and his long greasy fingers squiggled and scrunched in front of him, as if they were looking for a neck to go round. Dunstan saw him, and was just about to be frightened, when he realised he was too drunk and giggled instead. Macarius looked up and giggled also.

The sight of the two men sitting between the shelves giggling like idiots, sent Ronnie into a fit of rage, and he rabbled and railed and ruled like a tyrant, until he was red in the face with it. But the two men carried on giggling, so he sacked them.

CHAPTER THREE.

As they staggered out of the loading bay doors after clocking out, Macarius turned to Dunstan.

– Dunstan? he said.

– Yes? Dunstan said.

– If there really is a GOD, how come we got sacked?

Dunstan looked at Macarius.

– That's a stupid question, he said.

– Why?

– Because that's not what GOD's there for.

– What?

– Stopping people from getting sacked.

– Well, what *is* HE there for then?

– Bigger things.

– What kind of bigger things?

– All kinds of bigger things!

Macarius thought for a moment.

– Allright then, he said, If there really is a GOD, how come six million Jews got killed in the War?

The sun shone down brightly, like a huge burning planet, and some birds twittered in the afternoon sky. Dunstan thought for a moment or two, but his brain was still messy with the Jack Daniels. He looked up at the sky, then down at the ground, and finally at Macarius.

– I don't know, he said, and they both went home to their wives.

The End.

To: Jubilee Stores,   Thu. 5th May '88.
    151 Meed Lane,
    Rushfield,
    Nr. Boltham.

Dear Sir,

I'm sorry my letter is so late, but unfortunately my mother used the newspaper with your advert in it to wrap up the potato peelings, before I'd had a chance to read it. I went round to my Grandma's house, but the paperboy had caught glandular fever from not wearing enough clothes, and her copy had not been delivered. My uncle Brian usually has a copy, but he is in Torremolinos for two weeks and has cancelled his papers. Even if he hadn't, I couldn't get in because I don't have a key.

So I went to the Chronicle Office the day after and asked them for a back issue, but they had none left. The woman, (Beryl I think she was called), said they usually had loads, but there had been a technical hitch, and not as many copies had been printed that day. I called at my Grandma's but her paper boy was still sick, and my uncle Brian was still away, and I couldn't think of where else to go.

It was purely by chance that I got an old copy of the paper, when my meat pie and chips came wrapped in it at dinner time today. I usually eat at home, but I was treating myself as I get my Giro on Thursdays. The jobs page was a bit greasy, but I managed to get your address, and this is why my letter is so late.

I would like to apply for the job of Warehouse Assistant please.

Yours sincerely,

Alan Tardy.

To: Alan Tardy,   Mon. 9th May '88.
   11 Fabian Street,
   Rushfield,
    Nr. Boltham.

Warehouse Assistant.

Dear Mr Tardy,

Thank you for your application for the above post. I'm sorry to have to tell you that the vacancy was filled almost a month ago.

However, we may well be advertising other vacancies in the not too distant future, so next time you see your mother peeling potatoes, I should make a beeline for the paper.

Yours sincerely,

Kevin Daughtry

Ass. Warehouse Manager.

To: Kevin Daughtry,   Wed. 11th May '88.
    c/o Jubilee Stores,
    151 Meed Lane,
    Rushfield.

Dear Kevin,

Thank you for your letter of 15th April about the job of Warehouse Assistant. It made a nice change to receive a personal reply as opposed to a photocopy with my name inserted, or worse still, nothing at all. (If you've ever been unemployed, you'll know what I mean).

As for tips on getting published, I should tell you that I am by no means an expert, and probably not the right person to ask. What I *would* suggest however, is that you try to decide what you do best, do it, and send it out to someone. I've talked to so many people who are full of wonderful ideas for stories they are going to write – just as soon as they get the time. I suspect that talking about it is as far as they'll ever get. If you're really serious about it, you have to *make* the time, and I believe the best way to find out if you're any good or not, (or saleable at any rate), is to put your ideas down on paper and send them to a publisher, (or literary agent). There is a comprehensive list of both in the Writer's and Artist's Yearbook.

My own tastes in literature are pretty varied, but since you expressed an interest, I've included below a brief list of the kind of things I've read and enjoyed. There are many omissions; these are just the ones that spring readily to mind. (Incidentally, I think it is important that you read people like Tolstoy, Fielding, Eliot, Dickens etc., since there are few effective literary devices that do not, in the first place, owe their existence to the classics.)

I hope this letter proves helpful, and I wish you the very best of British.

                    Yours with regards,

                    John Kirkbride.

Booklist.

Catch 22	Joseph Heller.
Portnoy's Complaint	Philip Roth.
Mila 18 (have tissues at the ready)	Leon Uris.
Road to Wigan Pier	George Orwell.
Down and Out in Paris and London	George Orwell.
A Rumour of War	Philip Caputo.
Delcorso's Gallery	Philip Caputo.
The Girl in the Swing	Richard Adams.
Weaveworld (nice prose)	Clive Barker.
Slaughterhouse 5	Kurt Vonnegut Jr.
Rise and Fall of the Third Reich	Richard L. Shirer.
To Kill a Mockingbird	Harper Lee.

I also suggest that you read Shakespeare's plays, and for light relief (though nimble prose) the work of Douglas Adams. And I can heartily recommend *anything* by Stephen King.

JKB

To: John Kirkbride,   Fri. 13th May '88.
     New Inn Farm,
     Highmoor,
     Nr. Oldham.

Dear John,

Thank you very much for your kind letter which arrived this morning. (My boss was dying to know what was in it, and has been giving me filthy looks all day). It was very good of you to write back, and your advice seems very sensible to me.

Also, my friend Chris (who works here) has got all the Stephen King books, and says he will bring some in on Monday for me to borrow. I have always been a bit septical about horror stories, but as you are an author yourself, I expect you know what you're talking about, so I'll give them a go.

Thanks again for the advice, and the best of British to you, too.

Yours with regards,

Kevin Daughtry

To: Kevin Daughtry,   Wed. 25th May '88.
     391 Boltham Road,
     Boltham.

Dear Kevin,

I'm sorry I haven't written back to you sooner, but I've been busy preparing a mid-term seminar, and I'm afraid I just haven't had time for anything else for the last couple of weeks.

However, I've now had a chance to read your latest story, (IN AMONG THE PALLET RACKS), and I think it's terrific. There's still room for grammatical and stylistic improvement of course, but I definitely think it's the best thing you've written so far. The influence of WAITING FOR GODOT was easy to detect, but doesn't detract from the story's intrinsic strength.

I think the concept of GOD inside a bottle of Jack Daniels is wonderful. I felt you were expressing the view that modern civilisation eschews the notion of Holy Sanctity, and instead, takes refuge in contemporary substitutes such as money, power, and ultimately of course, alcohol.

The dialogue I found particularly exciting, and the ending left me thoughtful and sad, as good literature should. You seem to have grasped the idea that the best stories do not necessarily have a 'storyline' as such, and nor do they need one, so long as the style is ambiguous and thought provoking. Always remember, a good book is hard to read, and the same goes for short stories.

Keep up the good work, and I look forward with anticipation to reading your next piece.

Ciao,

Joyce.

P.S. I thought the names, Dunstan and Macarius, were excellent, but I do wish you'd stop writing 'ha ha' at the end of sentences; it's beginning to grate.

Dear Diary,

The last few weeks have certainly turned out to be quite interesting, or bits of them anyway. On the Monday after Melanie and I spent the night together, we were both dead embarrassed at work, though I don't think anyone else noticed. She didn't seem to want to talk to me and I wondered if she thought I'd taken advantage of her. I'd apologise, only I can't remember what happened, so I might not have done anything wrong. The thing is, if Melanie can't remember either, then I say I'm sorry, she's going to *think* I did something wrong, and that's even worse! It doesn't really matter now anyway, as fate has taken a hand to stop us going out with each other. Her parents are moving back to Birmingham and Melanie's decided that she's going to go with them.

I got quite depressed about it when she told me, and went out last night to drown my sorrows, when who should I meet in Chuzzlewit's, but Marci Niland, the girl who came in for an interview at Jubbies! I couldn't believe it! I was out with Chris Stevens and Nev from work, and the bar was really packed, so we went upstairs and there she was, sitting with two of her mates. She recognized me from Jubbies, so we sat down with them and got chatting and me and Marci got on like a hay loft on fire, ha ha. Her hair was fastened up in a sort of 'thing' on top, and she had lipstick on and everything, and the lads were dead impressed. The drag was, her and her mates were going to Yates's Wine Lodge to see some friends – BUT!! – she agreed to meet me in Chuzzlewit's to 8 o'clock tonight! I've been biting my fingernails all day.

At work last week, I got another official warning from The King, because he keeps finding me reading when I'm supposed to be working, and I've been using Jubbies stationary and typewriter to write my stories. I'll have to watch my step.

Speaking of stories, I have made an important discovery. Stephen King is the best writer in the world! I've read three of his books already, and the one I've just finished (called 'IT') is absolutely brilliant. It's like Lord of the Rings set in modern day America. I've now decided I'd like to start writing proper stories instead of simplistic intellectual narratives. I think there might be more of a market for them anyway.

I just hope Joyce won't be too upset, as she thought IN AMONG THE PALLET RACKS was the best thing I'd written. I thought so too until I showed it to Chris at work. He thought it was rubbish, and I must admit when I reread it, it did sound a bit daft. I really don't know where Joyce got all that stuff about 'modern civilisation' and 'Holy Sanctity'. Even *I* didn't know that was what it meant.

Anyway, I'm working on something now with a proper storyline to it, and I'm going to take the advice of that author who wrote to me, and send it off. I've found this magazine in W. H. Smith's called 'The Mind's Eye', which is full of all kinds of weird stories, so I might send it there.

Well, that's about all for now. Will keep you posted on further developments with Marci.

Sat. 28th May '88.

To: Joyce Beckett,   Thu. 2nd June '88.
     36 R.D. Laing Street,
     Canterbury.

Dear Joyce,

Thank you for your letter of 25th May. I'm really glad you liked IN AMONG THE PALLET RACKS.

However, I hope you will not be too disappointed when I tell you that I have decided to change direction, and steer away from the more simplistic intellectual fields, to concentrate on something a bit more commercial. Even though I found the books you recommended quite interesting, I must admit I had to force myself to keep reading them, as they weren't very exciting, and a couple of times I fell asleep behind the canned fruit shelves at work. Also, I had to keep looking things up in the dictionary all the time, and even then, I couldn't understand what it all meant. I suppose that's because I'm not very intellectual, unlike yourself.

Anyway, my latest story is completely different from the previous ones, and in my opinion, it is the best thing I have written. (It certainly *took* longer than any of the others!) I hope you enjoy reading it, and are not too upset by my change of style.

I look forward to hearing your views.

Ciao,

Kevin Daughtry

P.S. I have also sent a copy of the story to 'The Mind's Eye' magazine, so I will let you know what happens.

See You Tomb Horror.

EGYPT, 1921.

Conway and Professor Howard looked at each other and scratched their heads. In despite of all their careful plans and calculations, (written on some beer mats in an old bizarre in Cairo), they had come to a complete dead end. Right where the entrance to the main chamber should have been, was a solid stone wall that nothing less than an industrial bulldozer would shift. All they had were two trowels and a sweeping brush.

Conway sat down in the dust and scratched his chin. His thick, black eyebrows furrowed and his long, pointed nose twitched, making him look like a large mouse on the trail of Edam.

'Shit,' he said, staring deep into the air in front of him.

'Where?!' said Professor Howard, dancing worriedly on the spot.

'Nowhere you bespectacled twit! I mean "shit" as in damn, or blast!'

'Ah,' said the Professor, 'I see. And indeed, I concur.'

'We must have got it wrong.'

'We do certainly seem to have come to a dead end.'

'Our calculations must have been out.'

'But I don't see how. I checked and re-checked them.'

'Yes, but that was after we'd spilt beer over them.'

'True.' said the Professor, and he put out his arm and leaned against the wall in a gesture of being fed up. Suddenly, one of the stones gave a click and the solid wall began to move.

'What the. . . . ?!' he cried, sounding like some twerp out of an old black and white horror movie, and Conway leapt to his feet. (His own feet, not the Professor's feet, ha ha).

'That's it!' he yelled, 'That's it! A secret door, of course!'

'Why yes, how obvious,' agreed the Professor, standing

back as the wall turned to reveal an opening, 'I mean, they would hardly put a neon sign over the entrance to a secret chamber, now would they?'

'Would they buggery!' said Conway, and the two men stood back and watched as the wall ground to a halt, revealing a large square opening of black darkness.

'It looks pretty dark,' whispered the Professor, peering into the gloom.

'What did you expect?' said Conway testicly, 'fluorescent strip lights?' The Professor coughed dismissively.

'We'd better light the oil lamps,' he said.

So they lit the oil lamps, and intrepidly but with ginger, they tiptoed through the opening and into the secret chamber, which no one had seen for over three thousand years, (except the cleaners, ha ha). As their lamps hit the darkness, it disappeared, and they were almost dazzled by the glittering jewels and shining gold ornaments that had been buried with King Tutanhotep all those years before. In fact, they *were* dazzled, and it took them a bit of a while to readjust their eyes.

When they could see again, they looked around in wonderment, and Conway whistled through his teeth, which if you've ever tried it, (as I have), you will know is quite difficult. Professor Howard sighed.

'Just think what a wonderful contribution to History this is going to make,' he said.

'Just think what a wonderful contribution to my *pocket* this is going to make!' Conway replied, laughing greedily.

The two men strided to the centre of the chamber where the gold coffin lay, surrounded by jewels and heavy statues, and began to examine their treasure. Suddenly, there was a loud grinding sound behind them, and they spun round just in time to see the huge stone wall sliding back into place. They made a run for it, but they both smoked and were a bit slow, and before they could reach it, the wall slammed shut with a resounding sound. They were sealed in the chamber. They looked at each other in fear, and all the greed fled like Christmas turkeys from Conway's eyes.

'We're trapped,' he said, sniffling and twitching and looking more than ever like a mouse.

'Hmm. It would appear that you are correct,' agreed the Professor, indulging in some surveylance of the chamber for signs of a way out. Conway began to scamper around the walls, tapping them and fondling the bricks, trying to find a secret mechanism or another hidden door, but there was none to be had.

Finally, after half an hour of searching, the two men sat down in the sand and handed in their resignations to fate.

'We should have known there would be some sort of device to protect the treasure,' said the Professor, 'Blimey, we've read enough adventure stories in our time!'

'I know,' said Conway hopelessly, 'I just never thought about it.'

As the lamps flickered in the ancient air, the two men closed their eyes, and before long, (about ten minutes or so), they were fast asleep. All of a sudden, there was a slight movement from the gold coffin in the centre of the chamber, and the lid began to slide off very slowly. It landed in the sand with an expensive thud, and the four eyes of the two men popped open as if someone had poked them with a pointed stick. Conway and the Professor stared with suspension of belief, as very, very slowly, the bandaged and tattered body of Tutanhotep began to rise from its ancient resting place. They cringed and quivered, as it climbed out of its coffin and stood wobbling on the sandy floor. (It wobbled because it hadn't stood up for three thousand years ha ha). Then slowly, like a drunk crossing his bedroom in the dark, the body began to walk across the chamber towards the secret door. When it got to the wall, it reached out one of its tattered arms and touched a stone that looked no different from any of the others. With a grinding, crunching, rumbling sound, the wall began to turn, and once more the secret opening was revealed.

The two men watched in amazement as the dead king turned around, walked back to his coffin and climbed in. Without saying a word, they leapt to their feet, rushed through the opening and down the passage, and out into the dazzling Egyptian sunlight.

By nine o'clock that night, after several large brandies and a pint of lager in the hotel bar, Conway and the Professor had just about stopped shaking. The Professor downed another brandy and lit his pipe.

'You realise of course what happened, ouch, this afternoon?' he said, shaking out his match and burning his fingers. Conway nodded, and swallowed his own brandy.

'Either we were dreaming, or we both had the same hallucination,' he said.

'A combination of the two I suspect,' the Professor went on, 'A joint, dreamlike hallucination, brought about by excess fatigue, and the shock of believing ourselves to be trapped forever in the tomb.'

'Yes,' Conway agreed, sipping his lager, 'That sounds perfectly reasonable to me. We both know there are no such things as walking mummies.'

'Quite so,' the Professor said. Conway thought about the gold and jewels they had left behind in the chamber.

'I think we should go back tomorrow and start bringing the stuff out,' he said.

'I agree. It will all look quite different after a good night's sleep,' and so saying, they finished their drinks and went to bed.

Next morning at 11am, after a hearty breakfast of eggs and camelburgers, the two men once again stepped into the ancient chamber, followed by some Egyptians they had employed to carry the stuff. They looked around a bit nervously, but nothing seemed to be out of place, and the lid of the coffin was shut tight, as it had been for the last three thousand years.

'Just as I thought,' said the Professor, 'A joint hallucination.'

'Better cut down on the joints then, hadn't we,' said Conway, laughing, but the Professor didn't get the joke.

'Probably a touch of sunstroke,' he said, and Conway stopped laughing and agreed.

'Yes,' he said, 'The sun can do strange things to a man.'

Just then, one of the Egyptian porters called out to them from across the chamber.

'Hey! Professor! What ees thees?' he said. The Professor wandered over to where the man was standing.

'What is what?' he said, blasely.

'Thees!' said the Egyptian, and he pointed exitedly at the sandy floor. There, leading from the coffin to the wall and back again, were the unmistakable footprints of King Tutanhotep's mummy. The Professor took one look, and fell over in a dead feint.

The End.

To: Jubilee Stores,   Mon. 6th June '88.
    151 Meed Lane,
    Rushfield,
    Nr. Boltham.

To whoever's in charge,

I have been told that you often advertise for warehouse staff, so I am writing to you for a job. I am 25 years old, very strong and pretty good looking into the bargain.

I have been out of work for a few months now, but this is only because I keep getting passed over for young 15 year old brats, who'll work for less money than me. (Suckers). Even though I'm very good in interviews – tell a few dirty jokes, shoot all the right bullshit – nobody seems to want to employ me. I reckon it's because they're worried I'll be too good for the job. Stupid buggers.

Anyway, as I've heard you're a very good company to work for, I'm sure you won't let this bother you. I will come in for an interview as soon as I hear from you, and by the way, even though I'm out of work I'm a busy man, so I'd appreciate it if you'd send me a reply as soon as possible.

Hugh Briss.

To: Hugh Briss,   Wed. 8th June '88.
    133 Crabby Street,
    Boltham.

Dear Mr Briss,

Thank you for your pleasant little application for a job
with Jubilee Stores.

However, we are not looking for any more people at
the moment and when we are, I think we'll just wait
until some cheap, 16 year old sucker comes along, and
employ *him*.

Thank you for your interest, and I'm not sorry I can't
be of more help.

Yours sincerely,

Kevin Daughtry

Ass. Warehouse Manager.

To: Kevin Daughtry,   Fri. 10th June '88.
    391 Boltham Road,
    Boltham.

Dear Kevin,

Thank you for sending me your latest effort, **SEE
YOU TOMB HORROR**. However, let me say at the
outset that I was rather disappointed to learn of your
change of direction, and, I have to say, more than a little
disappointed with the story itself. (The title is appalling).

It seems such a shame that after making such good
progress, you should have turned to this type of trivial
and banal sensationalism, which has neither literary or
intellectual merit to recommend it. Besides which, to be

brutally frank, I don't think you are a good enough writer to produce work of this kind of a saleable quality.

I'm afraid my main reaction to the piece was – so what? It does not fulfil any of the functions of the short story: there are no twists, it does not stand as a fine example of prose, nor does it provide meaningful insights into anything. The story is feeble and inconsequential, and the basic plot is so weak, I can't see what could be done to salvage it.

Quite apart from that, you obviously think you now know better than I do, since you are STILL using that pathetic little 'ha ha' device, to try and lend humour to lines which are not particularly funny. No publisher is going to look at a writer who uses such juvenile tricks.

Moreover, who wants to read about a couple of Egyptian archeologists, when they could be reading about the heroic struggle of artists and intellectuals, living in squalor, unknown and unappreciated in the backstreets of obscurity. People like James Joyce and Malcolm Lowry were not merely simple storytellers: they were innovators, and I had hoped that you might try to follow in their footsteps and experiment with the language, rather than simply 'utilise' it.

I'm sorry to say, if you're determined to carry on writing this kind of trivial nonsense, I can no longer be of any help to you. I think it would be a tragic waste of your potential talent, but the decision is yours of course.

Let me know if you change your mind.

Yours,

Joyce.

To: Kevin Daughtry,   Sat. 11th June '88.
    391 Boltham Road,
    Boltham.

Dear Kevin Daughtry,

Many thanks for sending us your short story, SEE
YOU TOMB HORROR. I very much liked the
humorous style of the piece, but I'm afraid I am unable
to accept it for publication.

As a pastiche, it is unusual and appealing, but THE
MIND'S EYE attempts to cater for the more serious
Science Fiction/Horror reader, and what we really need
is something rather more along those lines.

However, your writing shows promise, and you will no
doubt improve with practice, and I would be happy to
read more of your work in the future.

Manuscripts should be typed, preferably double
spaced, and of no more than 2500 words. Contents may
be on pretty well any subject, bearing in mind the type of
thing we publish. Payment is £100 per story, and is
payable on publication.

I look forward to future submissions.

                        Yours sincerely,

                            Nick Eldritch.

P.S. I loved the title of your story.

To: Kevin Daughtry.   Mon. 13th June '88.
    Warehouse.

Mr Daughtry,

It has come to my attention in recent weeks that your timekeeping and conduct at work have been less than satisfactory. I am also aware that you have been using company stationery etc. for the purposes of personal correspondence, and I'm afraid that this cannot be tolerated.

Having already issued three official warnings, I hereby give notice of the termination of your employment with this company, as of Friday 17th June.

Signed,

Elvis Jones.

Dear Diary,

Oh shit.

Mon. 13th June '88.

Dear Diary,

Woke up this morning with a terrible hangover. I went out with Melvin Snetterton last night because his dad's just got back from Lybia, where they've been holding him for the last six months on trumped up spy charges. What a joke! He wears jam jar bottoms for glasses, and wouldn't make a decent train spotter, let alone military spy! Anyway, they let him go last week and he got back here on Friday, so we went to Chuzzlewit's last night to celebrate. And boy, did we celerate! Why is it that having fun always seems to end up being painful?

I've just been checking back in my diary, and I was amazed to discover I've been out of work for over eight months now. Having said that, it's possibly been the most constructive eight months of my life. I've worked it out, and since I left Jubbies, I've read over sixty books, written twenty five short stories, fourteen poems and thirty two job applications, and for the last four months I've been going to English classes at nightschool twice a week. (It's free if you're on the dole). I've sent ten of my stories to various magazines but without much success so far, though Nick Eldritch, Assistant Editor at THE MIND'S EYE, keeps telling me to send more. He always gives me constructive criticism, and has really helped me improve my technique over the last few months. I've just finished a story about a flea, so if I can afford the postage, I'll send that tomorrow.

Things are still going great on the romantic front, (though the back leaves much to be desired, ha ha), and Marci and I are still getting on as well as ever, though I think she'll be glad when I start earning some money. (Frankly, she won't be the only one). There was a smidgen of acrimony last week after I got a letter from Melanie in Birmingham, and Marci found it in my jacket pocket. I had to take her to Butterfield's for a fish and chip supper to patch things up. I suppose I should have told her that Melanie and I keep in touch, but I thought it might cause more trouble than it was worth. Women are strange and unpredictable creatures. Come to think of it, so are men. That's probably why we get on so well.

Oh well; back to the typewriter. I just hope Nick Eldritch thinks my latest story is as good as *I* think it is.

NOTE: Remember to get Marci a Valentine's Card tomorrow.

Sun. 12th February '89.

To: Nick Eldritch,   Mon. 13th February '89.
    Pixie Publications,
    666 Dybbuk Street,
    London.

Dear Nick,

Thank you for your recent letter about my last story, KILLER HAMSTERS. On reflection, I think you are right about the subject matter being too bizarre to really be frightening. The bit where the leader of the hamsters eats Colonel Gadaffi's cat, just didn't ring true somehow.

However, I'm glad to hear that you think I'm 'getting there', and enclosed is a story which hopefully, will bear this out. It all fell into place quite easily somehow, and I've reread it a couple of times and still like it. I also took your advice about research, and read some 'Gun Mart' magazines and a handbook on psychology before writing it. It may not be Stephen King, but I think it's the best thing I've done so far. (And the 'Spellmaster' mini-computer I got for Christmas has impreved my spalling drumaticully, ha ha).

I hope you like the story, and look forward to hearing from you.

                    Best wishes,

                    Kevin Daughtry

The Flea.

He reached the T.V. just as it began to whistle, and switched it off before it could disturb him. The piercing whine after the programmes ended irritated him immensely, and he often pondered the – to him – horrific idea of being tied to a chair in a room with a whistling television set. He was in no doubt that it would simply drive him completely out of his tree.

He walked back and checked that the front door was locked and that he had put the cat out, (it didn't like being on fire, ha ha)., and turning off the lights, made his way upstairs to his bedroom. He switched on his reading lamp and sat down on the edge of the bed.

It hadn't been a bad day from his point of view. Perhaps for the people he'd interviewed on behalf of the Inland Revenue, it hadn't been so good, but for him, not bad. Lunch with Walker had been quite enjoyable, even if Walker was a trifle too liberal in his outlook, and the afternoon had passed agreeably enough, helped no doubt, by the two medium sherries he had drunk along with his grilled Dover sole and salad.

Arnold Sissons was a fairly likeable sort of man, though one or two of his colleagues at the I.R. found him a little stuffy. Perhaps he was, but he would have been unable to do anything about it even if he had been aware of it, which he was not. It wasn't pomposity so much as an innate sense of conservatism, distilled into him by his parents who raised him to be reserved, polite, punctual and above all, clean. Cleanliness is, after all, next to Godliness.

He viewed all things radical with the kind of unease that is rooted in a deep fear of change. His childhood had been strict, routined, ordered, and he had vigorously – or with as much vigour as his character would allow – pursued these virtues into adult life. Another child might have rebelled and gone the other way, but not Arnold.

He knew better than that. He thought he knew in which direction lay happiness and contentment, a delusion probably caused by the fact that he had never really experienced either, ha ha.

He smiled to himself as he remembered one of Walker's lunchtime comments, and turning back the bedcovers, he began to get undressed. He reached down and took off his left shoe, (always the left shoe first), and there, near the toe of his pale cream coloured sock, was a tiny, black insect.

He didn't realise it was an insect at first, but just as he was about to brush it away with a sweep of his hand, it moved slightly to one side. He withdrew the hand quickly and instinctively with a slight shudder of revulsion. Recovering himself, he bent carefully to inspect the creature more closely, pushing his hornrimmed spectacles back on his nose from where they frequently slipped, one of the arms having been repaired with a short piece of plastic and Epoxy Resin. The insect looked familiar in a nasty sort of way. He was sure he'd seen it before, or something very like it. In an encyclopedia, or a biology book perhaps. This idea triggered a sudden recognition and he recoiled again, this time with something more like horror than revulsion.

It was a flea.

It jumped, and landed a little higher up on his sock. He felt goosepimples emerge over his body, like blisters in new paint on a hot July afternoon, and was vaguely aware of a cool sweat breaking out on his brow and in the smalls of his back. This was dreadful, simply dreadful. Even worse than a whistling television. Because this was alive. This was a living creature, an insect, a *flea*, and noticing a cluster of small, dark red spots on his shin above the sock, one that was living quite nicely thank you, off *his* blood! It had punctured his skin with its specially designed mouth, had injected its anti-clotting saliva to prevent the blood from hardening, and had sucked it greedily up into its body, like a child might suck Coca-Cola through a straw. The thought caused an involuntary shiver, and with a feeling of sudden anger and disgust, he struck out wildly at the insect, which hopped easily out of harm's way and landed. . . .

. . . . Somewhere else.

The foul disgusting little creature had disappeared. It was no longer on his sock. He rolled up his trouser leg quickly and examined the fine brown hairs and pale skin of his lower leg. There! That mark. He looked closer, but it was a tiny mole. He'd never noticed it before, but there it was. He brushed it with a finger to make sure, but it was definitely nothing more than a blemish. Clutching his leg in both hands, he pulled it upwards until it was only inches from his nose, and peered at it. He could see nothing. The flea was gone – but where? Even now, his imagination told him, it was doubtless burrowing through some tiny gap in the fabric – a buttonhole perhaps, or the worn lining of his trouser pocket – searching for a tasty looking expanse of human flesh into which to sink its evil sucking device.

Arnold was terrified of insects. He was mollified by the idea of being stung by a bee, or a wasp, and if he saw a spider crawling over the carpet – even if they did kill flies – he would stamp on it and meticulously scrub the area with disinfectant. He was frightened of moths and of the things that bumped against the windows in the night, and on his one and only trip abroad, had worked his way through five tubes of Flypel insect repellent in an effort to keep the mosquitoes away. In desperation, he had put on a pullover and scarf, ha ha.

But fleas!

Fleas were disgusting, blood-sucking, ugly creatures. Nothing was uglier than a flea, with its squat misshapen body and its long jointed legs, legs that would propel it several feet in one jump. It had probably come in from the cold with the cat as its host. Or it could be the human flea, pulex irritans, (he had read up on his insects, yesiree), which specialises in living off human blood. And you can't crush a flea between your fingers; they're too tough. Chase one off, and it lies in wait nearby for the chance to hop back on. A *flea* of all things! The same creature that spread the bubonic plague from rats to humans, and wiped out over a third of the population of 14th Century Europe.

And now the same insect was on *him*; wriggling about somewhere in his clothes, looking for the right spot to insert its horrible mouth and begin another banquet of human blood. And as soon as the blood hardened in one spot, the flea would hop to another and start all over again. The very idea was odorous.

He felt a tickle on his spine and almost cried out, before he recognised it as a rolling bead of sweat. He stood up quickly, panic now tapping insistently at the back of his conscious mind, and batted wildly and unreasonably at himself and his clothes. He danced stupidly from one foot to the other, watching the pale grey carpet beneath him, as if expecting a motley collection of unloosened fleas to tumble onto it from his body. But none appeared. He rushed over to his wardrobe and rummaged in the bottom until he came up with a plastic carrier bag. Striding back across the room, he began tearing off his clothes and stuffing them into the bag. He was by now almost hysterical. He was sweating profusely and breathing fast, and every now and then he would emit a low moan, as if his very life depended upon his stripping in time.

He was suddenly aware of a slight tickling sensation on the back of his left thigh.

He stiffened, like an earthling caught in an alien death-ray, his shirt pulled open to reveal a pale and hairless starling chest. He stayed in this position for several seconds, waiting for the sensation to come again, and when it did, he ripped the shirt (one of his best) off completely, and began clutching and batting at his trouser leg as if it had suddenly and inexplicably caught fire.

All over his body now he could feel an itching and pricking, as every hair on the surface of his skin stood on end, and the flesh crawled beneath it. Or was it the flea crawling, weaving its way around his pores, looking for virgin territory on which to begin another sanguinary meal? Or were there more than one? Two perhaps, or three or four? He clutched crazily sat his head as his scalp began to itch. There could be dozens of them, hiding in his thick, curly hair, sucking at the blood vessels, draining them, licking their lips like vultures over a rotting carcass. He had once seen photographs in a magazine of a blood-sucking tick, before and after feeding, the 'before' picture of a small and harmless looking insect, the 'after' one, a huge, purple, bloated creature, its skin stretched tight and membranous as if about to burst.

He couldn't stand it. The thought of these monsters on his body was too much. He tore off his trousers and ran over to his desk in the corner of the room. With one hand he fumbled with the drawer key, scratching at his head with the other, then rubbing fanatically at his arms and the backs of his legs. His whole body felt like a lice-infested horsehair mattress.

He was, though he was too preoccupied to be aware of it, stumbling ungracefully over the edge, past the point where he could reach out and cling on to the last defiant branches of his sanity. Sweat was rolling off his forehead and down his temples. His breathing was erratic, his chest tight, like a marathon runner who has pushed too far beyond the pain barrier. He was whimpering now, the tears in the corners of his eyes a prelude to the sobs that would shortly take over. He could feel the fleas crawling over his back, his arms, his legs, hopping about in his hair, piercing his skin and sucking his blood.

At last he managed to unlock the drawer, and pulling it open, he stared inside with a mixture of fear, triumph and more than a dash of creeping insanity. His brain was simply not equipped to deal with the situation. Had it been anything other than insects, it might have been different, but Arnold Sissons was a hopeless entomophobic. He reached into the drawer and pulled out the Smith & Wesson Combat Model .357 Magnum. It had been a present from his cousin in Wisconsin, and had prompted him to make several visits to a local gun club before he lost interest. They had all been Gung Ho types, and Arnold could never understand their cavalry attitude to these devastating lethal weapons. Also, despite protective earphones, the noise had bothered him.

Now, he weighed the gun intently in his hand. It felt cold, heavy and powerful. Slowly, the anxiety and hysteria began to ebb, began rolling back like early morning mist, leaving his body ice cold and his mind needle-sharp with purpose. That this clear minded resolve was itself an abberation, was now well beyond the grasp of his traumatised brain. His lips peeled back from his teeth in what could have been a tormented smile or a grimace of pain. He stood by his desk, naked except for a pair of cream coloured socks and pale blue Y fronts, the revolver held firmly in his sweat-slimy right hand, and stared unblinkingly at nothing. If some unsuspecting cleaning woman had stumbled in on him, she would have screamed. He stood this way for several minutes, acutely aware of every inch of his flesh, every centimetre of skin, microscopically aware of every pore.

He waited.

Sure enough, he felt the now familiar pricking sensation on the upper part of his left foot, and the sickening grin widening across his face, he lowered his head and looked down. There, like a tiny ink spot on a blank page, was the flea, nesting comfortably in the woollen fabric of his sock. Moving carefully so as not to disturb it, he took a small cardboard box from the drawer, and loaded six .38 Special centre-fire cartridges into the revolver. With tears now rolling down his face and hands shaking, he began quietly to giggle, then lowering the gun, he pointed it at his sock. Struggling to hold it steady, he closed his eyes and fired. The retort echoed briefly and deafeningly around the room. The bullet smashed through his foot, fragmenting bone and spreading flesh, and embedded in the floorboard where it crossed the wooden joist beneath. Pain seared up his leg like flames along petrol, and he staggered back, his breath coming in short bursts, interspersed with strange guttural noises which sounded oddly like laughter. He gazed down in astonishment at the bloody mess that had moments earlier been his foot, and the smell of cordite and burning flesh drited up into his flaring nostrils.

His eyes began to blur with the tears, and at the edge of his peripheral vision, he noticed a swarm of tiny black dots. Hundreds of them. There was, of course, only one explanation: more fleas. Now they were everywhere, on the wall, on the ceiling; everywhere he looked there were fleas. He brought the gun up, clutching his right hand with his left to steady it, and fired into the wall over his bed. Plaster disintegrated and fell onto the pillow, and a small dust cloud formed where the bullet had entered the wall. He staggered from the recoil and stepped back on his shattered foot, the pain, like an electric shock, almost toppling him.

'Bastards!' he cried out, in a hoarse whisper; then louder, 'Bastards!'

He fired twice more at the wall, the second bullet glancing off the raught iron bedstead and ricochetting crazily through the large front window, leaving shards of broken glass on the carpet. He was vaguely aware of voices outside. Someone was screaming; someone else was shouting, and there was the sound of footsteps running along the pavement in front of the house.

'Bastards!' he screamed again, and pumped two shots into the carpet around his feet in case they were creeping up on him. The gun clicked impotently on the third shot, and he hobbled over to the desk, dragging his bloody foot behind him. He fumbled with the box of cartridges and slotted six more into place. Turning to face the room again and leaning on the desk for support, he held the gun out in front of him, clutching it tightly in both hands as they had shown him at the gun club. He regarded the room suspiciously, his eyes darting rapidly from side to side, images magnified and made double by his tears.

Like a swarm of tiny bees the black spots returned, hovering above him, gathering around the lightshade in the centre of the room. Suddenly alarmed again, he raised the Magnum and fired twice into the ceiling, plaster dust falling in plumes from the ragged bullet holes. He fired again, and heard a metallic 'thunk' as the shot pierced the water tank in the roof. A drip appeared over his dressing table, and was quickly replaced by a steady trickle.

'I'll drown the little bloodsuckers!' he thought crazily, and giggled.

The back wall of the bedroom began to pulsate, a deep, throbbing blue. Somewhere at the back of his mind he was aware of a familiar sound, odd and wailing, but he was unable to place it. By this point, another section of his brain had taken over, shutting down and sealing off rationality in a vain attempt to protect itself from the shock it was undergoing. But it was already too late. Sanity would never have returned to this man, even if he'd lived. Although he had always assumed the opposite to be true, he had been teetering on the edge all of his ordered life. All he needed was the push.

He suddenly noticed the shattered front pane, and a new wave of cold panic flooded over him. He hobbled over to the window, like some grotesquely funny horror movie actor, and glared out into the darkness. The strange pulsating indigo coalesced into a blue flashing police light, but by now, he was too far gone to understand the significance of this. He pointed the gun through the jagged hole in the glass.

'You won't get in through here you little bastards!' he screamed, and emptied the Smith & Wesson into the cold night air.

With the incandescence of a religious vision, a powerful searchlight beam ripped through the dark and temporarily blinded him. He raised his hands, still clutching the gun, and tried to cover his eyes. There was a single sharp crack, and he felt as if somebody had reached through the window and punched him hard in the solar plexus. He staggered backwards on his ruined foot and toppled over, Arnold lay on his back, staring wide-eyed at the ceiling and trying to breath, but his lungs wouldn't seem to work properly. He tried to sit up, and found he was suddenly very weak. He could hear someone shouting outside, but couldn't tell what they were saying. It all seemed so very distant and far away. He thought he heard the front door bang downstairs, but he couldn't be sure. It didn't seem important anyway. He was very tired. Couldn't remember ever being as tired as this. He closed his eyes. A nap would be nice. Very nice indeed. Perhaps that would stop his foot hurting.

Officer Browning leaned over the body with a faint look of distaste on his face. His young colleague, Jansen, stood a few feet away, pale, and shaking slightly. Browning removed the revolver from Arnold's hardening fingers, and whistled quietly.

'.357 Magnum,' he said appreciatively, 'Combat Model by the look of it.'

'What's a bloke like that doing with a Magnum?' Jansen asked, his voice strained and thin.

'Search me,' said the other, dropping the weapon into a small polythene sack, 'Just another loony I reckon.' He stepped over the body and approached the bag of clothes by the bed. 'Better check for some I.D. I s'pose.'

'D'you think we ought to touch those?' said Jansen quickly, nodding towards the carrier bag Browning had picked up.

'Why shouldn't we?'

'Well, hadn't we better leave them 'till the forensic lads get here?'

'I'm only going to look in his jacket for a wallet.'

'Yeah, but I mean, you never know what the guy might've had.'

'Like what?'

'I dunno, like, fleas or something.'

'Fleas?!'

'Well, you never know. He was a weirdo.'

'So's the Super, but he ain't got fleas.'

'Yeah, well, just don't bring 'em near me, that's all.'

'What's the matter with you?'

Jansen looked around as if to make sure he wasn't being overheard.

'Listen, don't say anything to the lads,' he said, 'But I'm an entomophobic.'

'A what?!' Browning wanted to know.

'It means I'm scared of insects. I know it sounds stupid, but I can't help it. They bring me out in a cold sweat. 'Specially blood-suckers like fleas.'

'Okay, okay, you stay over there then. *I'll* check his clothes.'

So the young PC stood by the body and watched as Browning fumbled inside the jacket pocket, and thus it was, that Janson failed to notice as the flea transferred itself effortlessly from Arnold's head, to his regulation black police sock.

To: Kevin Daughtry,   Wed. 22nd February '89.
    391 Boltham Road,
    Boltham,
    Lancs.

Dear Kevin,

Thank you for sending us your latest story, THE
FLEA. We would be pleased to offer you £100 First
British Serial Rights for the piece, and would like to run
it in our May edition of THE MIND'S EYE. If you are
in agreement, let me know, and we'll try and put through
payment as soon as possible.

I very much liked the style of this one (though I still
had to make one or two corrections), and if you can come
up with more work of this quality, I see no reason why
your stories shouldn't start appearing in the magazine on
a regular basis.

I'm so glad that this has worked out. Well done, and I
look forward to hearing more from you soon.

                    Best wishes,

                        Nick Eldritch.

To: Joyce Beckett,
    36 R.D. Laing Street,
    Canterbury.

Fri. 24th February '89.

Dear Joyce,

    Ha ha.

           Ciao,

           Kevin Daughtry

Michael Hardcastle
No Defence
Where does a brilliant, young footballer go for his kicks?
0 233 97912 3

Minfong Ho
Rice Without Rain
Famine in a Thai village make an insecure background for Ned and Jinda's uneasy romance.   0 233 97911 5

Rhodri Jones
Slaves and Captains
A version of Herman Melville's *Benito Cereno*, the true story of an 18th century slave ship and the strange events that occur on it.   0 233 98356 2

Different Friends
It was learning the truth about Azhar that shocked Chris into changing his attitude to love, making him think for the first time what the word really meant.   0 233 98096 2

Getting It Wrong
If you're young and black, it is very easy to 'get it wrong' as Clive and Donovan find out.   0 233 97910 7

Hillsden Riots
What happens when the frustrations of young black people become intolerable.   0 233 97827 5

Pete Johnson
Catch You On the Flip Side
A sharp, lighthearted look at what happens to a boy, accustomed to girls falling for him, when he falls in love himself.
0 233 98074 1

Secrets from the School Underground
To find out what's really going on at Farndale Comprehensive you have to 'read' the writing on the wall behind the bike shed – a sort of unofficial school newspaper.   0 233 97987 5

Geraldine Kaye
Great Comfort
Comfort Kwatey Jones is half British and half Ghanaian. She loves being in Ghana, but when she goes to stay with her grandmother there, she discovers that she does not know the country and its traditions as well as she imagines.
0 233 98300 7

A Breath Of Fresh Air
Amy's interest in a school project on slavery becomes a reality when she slips back in time to experience life as a black slave in eighteenth century Jamaica.   0 233 98163 2

John Kirkbridge
In Reply to Your Advertisement
Kevin Daughtry may not have a job but he is a persistent and imaginative letter writer and through his application letters and the replies he receives we get to know him more and like him better.   0 233 98344 9

Thank You For Your Application
Kevin Daughtry, once an unemployment statistic, now has a job and ambitions to write. Efforts to be 'great' result in rejections, but a more popular style seems likely to win through.   0 233 98446 1

Elisabeth Mace
Under Seige
The fantasy world of a sohisticated board game becomes an obsession with Morris Nelson and the characters involved in the game more important than the people around him.
0 233 98345 7

Beware the Edge
The perils of dabbling in the supernatural.   0 233 97908 5

Boxes
Rona Goodall is an old maid of eighteen and desperate for a boyfriend. Along comes Sean and her problems seem to be solved.   0 233 97670 1

Suzanne Newton
I Will Call It Georgie's Blues
Bitter family tension threatens the youngest son of a preacher in the American Deep South. 0 233 97720 1

Eduardo Quiroga
On Foreign Ground
A young Argentinian soldier in the Falklands remembers his love affair with an English girl. 0 233 97909 3

Lorna Read
The Lies They Tell
Ann is an ordinary teenager until a blow to the head leaves her with thought-reading powers and the knowledge that a prospective candidate is lying to the electorate. Proving it turns her into a temporary celebrity. 0 233 98444 5

Caryl Rivers
Virgins
A bitter-sweet story of American high school girls growing up in the fifties. 0 233 97791 0

Michael Rosen
The Deadman Tapes
Paul Deadman's curiosity is aroused by eight remarkable tapes, apparently the confessions and life stories of a group of young people. Who are these young people? Where are they now? Did they know each other? Who made the tapes? 0 233 98443 7

Margaret Simpson
The Drug Smugglers
Paul decides to track down the drug pushers who are supplying his sister.   0 233 97673 6

Andy Tricker
Accidents Will Happen
The author's own moving account of a motorbike accident which left him paralysed, and his struggle to regain a measure of independence.   0 233 98095 4

Rosemary Wells
The Man in the Woods
Is he an ordinary hooligan or a more sinister figure mysteriously connected with events of the American Civil War of a hundred years ago?   0 233 97785 6

When No One Was Looking
Young American tennis star, Kathy Bardy, resents her new rival but she didn't expect her to die.   0 233 97669 8